Harper -
Enjoy life -
Reading . . .
♡TBDoherty

Bread for the Table

Tara Botel Doherty

Pinehurst Literary Press

LOS ANGELES, CALIFORNIA

Pinehurst Literary Press Los Angeles, California taraboteldoherty.com

Publisher's Note: This is a work of fiction. Names, characters, places, and incidents are a product of the author's imagination. Locales and public names are sometimes used for atmospheric purposes. Any resemblance to actual people, living or dead, or to businesses, companies, events, institutions, or locales is completely coincidental.

Book Layout ©2017 BookDesignTemplates.com

Ordering Information: Quantity sales. Special discounts are available on quantity purchases by corporations, associations, and others. For details, contact the "Special Sales Department" at the address above.

Bread for the Table/ Tara Botel Doherty—1st ed.

ISBN: 978-0-9984647-0-1 (paperback) ISBN: 978-0-9984647-1-8 (eBook)

Critical Acclaim for Bread for the Table

A Story of Courage

...Bread for the Table is an inspiring story of one girl's fight to overcome the truth of her past, while she steers herself towards a healthy future, and deals with even the most painful truths of a life shaped by a series of misfortunes, and painful obstacles.

Doherty's prose is graceful, raw, delicate and yet sharply intuitive, and I found the story incredibly compelling! Great read.

- *Nicole D'Settēmi, Author of "Addictarium"*

Bread for the Table is a beautiful story!

...of how one woman has built her life on the memories of days gone by. Sage is a character who is easy to connect with as she takes you on her journey of her life. Through her eyes, you see the struggles that she has had to endure in order to make it this far.

Tara Botel Doherty is an exceptional author who knows how to write a very compelling story. This is my first experience with this author and I was deeply impressed with her smooth flowing writing style. I felt an immediate connection to her work. I feel this book is a great contribution to the literary world.

- *Suzie Housley, Midwest Book Review*

Lingers in one's Psyche.

This sensitive story takes the reader back to the 1990's in Los Angeles, California through the thoughts and attitudes of the main character, Sage. Though a college graduate of a prestigious university, she works temporarily as a waitress in a downtown deli. Crystal scenes, delicately, defined characters, and distinctive dialogue shown in flashbacks and poignant references to John Steinbeck sway the reader into Sage's life situations of abandonment, alienation, and physical abuse. Bread for the Table lingers in one's psyche. In the end, life changes and hope reigns. One hopes to read more of Sage's story.

- *Beth Martin Brown of "The Little Witch of Wichita"*

To P and R . . . with love.

Life is short, art is long.

~Seneca

One

THE SHARP BODY JERK brought me back. I was stuck in a white picket fence nightmare, complete with an enameled barbeque in the back yard and chimes hanging off of the front porch. Then the body jerk snapped me like a new piece of Tupperware. I was falling down an elevator shaft and laughing as my weight brought me closer, my arms stretched out to stop me from arriving at my final destination, a Norman Rockwell portrait. A picture which I will never be a part of, and that brings me back to where I am. No voo doo magic or miracles, but in my bed, between my sheets, and next to him. In the blue twilight of the early morning I am under something. It is lodged under my chin and against my windpipe. It is heavy. I cannot breathe. It is the thick, dark-haired arm of my boyfriend, Tomas. I lift his extremity and open my eyes to the fuzziness of the cold morn- ing. The light of the alarm clock reveals that I have five more minutes of sleep before I must get out of bed. As I turn around in bed to get more comfortable, Steinbeck, our Dalmatian, wakes up and starts to lick his hot spot raw, vibrating the mat- tress. It is the same hot spot that he has nursed throughout the summer blaze of pink lemonade and open windows in this empty house. The jingle sound of his steel dog collar and license interrupt the silence

1

of my five minutes. He walks in slow circles, making a place for himself, taking his paws and trying to smooth the folds of the sheets. I kick him off the bed. He walks down the hallway, and into the front room. I sink into the crushed polyester of my pillow, and feel around under it for the crumbled postcard of Disneyland, with smiling faces and waving hands. The lotus-pink lipstick kiss is imprinted on the smiles where the money from the tooth fairy should have been twenty-five years ago.

The alarm goes off. I turn on my back and prop my hands under my head, listening. The whining sound of the alarm doesn't wake Tomas. I look over at him. He sleeps. His dirty black hair curls around his face, flattened against the pillow. His large smile is covered by two lips dropping saliva onto the pillow case. I reach across him to turn off the alarm and brush against his sleep filled body. His muscular outline is perfect through the sheets. I move the bleached white sheet away from his body, just to look. The simmering scent of sex, sweat, and patchouli escapes from his pores. There are three finger nail scratches on the right side of his back. I was asleep when he came home last night and woke only long enough for him to grab me and pull my body close to his, two spoons in a silver setting from a hope chest. He turns his head in my direction, and I drop the sheet.

"What are you doing?" Tomas asks. "Nothing," I reply. He wipes the dried saliva off his mouth. "Don't you have to go to work?" he asks. "Yes, I do," I say. "Sage, can you take Steinbeck for a walk?" he asks. "I want to sleep in."

"It's going to make me run late," I whine. "Just take him out to pee," he orders. Tomas looks at me with his black eyes. "Yeah, I'll do it'" I concede. "What's wrong, Sage?" he asks. "Nothing." "I can read your face," he chides. I take the card out from under the pillow. The same place I always put my lost

2

teeth and waited for my dollar from the tooth fairy when I was a child. As I hand the postcard to him, my hand looks so child-like.

"What is it?" he asks, sitting up in the bed. He moved the sheet to cover his bare body.

"A postcard from my mother," I answer. "I thought she was dead, Sage," he says. "I haven't heard from her since I was a kid," I sit close to him and touch his calf.

"Don't do that, Sage," he raises his voice in an authoritative tone.

"What should I do, Tomas?" I ask. I touch his calf feeling the warmth of his body.

"Stop touching me and go to work. Forget about it. It's probably nothing. You always worry about everything. Don't think it to death," he chides.

"You're right," I say listening to his tongue-lash. I sit on the bed with the postcard grasped in my right hand. As I look into the beautiful black eyes of this man in my bed, I lean my body in closer to his. To feel the warmth of another person's body is always powerful.

He turns around and lies back down in the bed. His face is away from me, tucked neatly on the pillow.

I hear the slow regulation of his quiet snore begin. He is asleep.

There is a cold snap throughout the house. I get out of bed and leave the sheet where it falls. Listening to the dog in the front room licking his hot spot with enthusiasm, I walk into the bathroom and turn on the uncovered light. I keep meaning to put the glass fixture back over the bulb, but I can't get the fit right. It slides off and tilts because I can't get the fifth screw in correctly, just can't thread it properly. I sit on the cold plastic of the toilet seat and reach across to an empty toilet tissue roll.

There is nothing but the brown cardboard and fragments of white paper glued to the end of the roll. I reach above to the box of seafoam green Kleenex tissue on the lid of the toilet.

Tomas once said it bothered him that bathrooms were designated in the colors of blue and pink. He said that a bathroom shouldn't be gender specific. It should be filled with asexual items like sea shells picked up on a warm October afternoon, while chasing the waves with someone you care about. I agreed with his words because I liked him so much. Every word he said became a part of my own Bible.

I stand in front of the mirror and talk to myself. "I look so old. There are lines in the fine skin under my eyes. I used to look so young. I'm only the other side of thirty."

In the other room, I hear Tomas cough into the open air. When I am not in the bed, he sleeps in a fetal position. He is childlike, down to the loopy handwriting and block letters he uses when he writes me notes. I used to spend my nights staring at his beauty while he slept. We've been together five years this month.

Five years ago, this month, I was sitting on the sidewalk in a hard steel chair at a plastic table reading. I was reading Cannery Row, *the only link I have to my father. My grandmother said he only read books by John Steinbeck. He had the entire collection. He would read them all, and then when he was finished, he would begin again. He never did read a newspaper, Grandma said. "Filled with the misery of other people," he told her when she asked him if he had read the paper that day.*

I was sitting on the sun-filled sidewalk of the Dutch American Bakery on Glendale Boulevard in Atwater next to Bill's Liquor Store. I like to sit and watch the morning alcoholics shiver in the front doorway as they stand and count their change in the palms of their hands. A woman in a tangerine cardigan and blue jeans emerged from the store with a brown bag held between her two hands in prayer. I was drinking a cup of coffee and eating a sticky pecan roll. A beautiful man walked by me with dense black curls and a strong mouth. He turned up the sides of his mouth in a small smile as he caught my eye. Then he disappeared through the glass door ringing the entry bell. I escaped back into the link with my father and the words he so admired. I was looking at the notes my father had written in the margins of the page. I only read the dog-eared copies which my father left behind.

"Excuse me," he said "sorry." The beautiful man bumped my chair as he wove around to the empty table next to my table.

"That's OK," I said nervously. An ambulance raced up the boulevard, flashing red lights and sounding a piercing alarm. As it passed by me, I made the sign of the cross. I felt the beautiful man stare at me.

"Catholic?" he asked. "Yes," I answered blushing. "I believe the sign of the cross is an inbred thing," he replied. "It might be," I confirmed. I read the same line about Dora Flood three times. I looked up at the beautiful man. He was reading a book The Grapes of Wrath.

One of five memories I have of my father was his reading The Grapes of Wrath to me as I sat on his lap. He would speak the words as if by memory, each one rolling out of his mustached mouth. I would sit there, hearing the rhythm of the words float on the air from his dark and melodious voice. As he came to the last paragraph of The Grapes of Wrath, he cleared his voice and sat in a moment of silence. I bowed my head in a five-year-old prayer. He read the paragraph with tears in his eyes, repeating the last two words "smiled mysteriously" two times. Then he closed the book and closed his eyes.

"Do you like Steinbeck?" the beautiful man asked. "Memories," I replied. He looked at me. I saw his full face against the shadow of the sun. Black curls wisped around his face and deep black eyes. He had wide Native-American cheekbones and inch-long black eyelashes. He was beautiful, almost pretty.

"Hello," he said. "Hello," I said. "My name is Tomas," he said standing up. He held his hand out to me.

5

"My name is Sage," I said taking it. His hand was smooth to the touch, visually flawless and pleasantly warm.

I look in the mirror and I think of that gypsy day five years ago. I turn on the water in the sink, and try to balance the hot side of the faucet with the cold side. In this old house, the pipes take a long time to warm up. I turn on the shower. A banging noise comes from the basement where the hot water heater is located. The pipes clear, and the steam rises throughout the bathroom clouding up the mirror. I soak my tattered, bleached-white washcloth and wash away the wrinkle cream I spent twenty dollars on during a day of vanity. The pipes make a noise and I turn off the sink. The soap residue comes off in my hand when I open up the shower door. I drape a towel across the door and drop my T-shirt on the floor.

The burning temperature of the water feels good against my back. I use the French-milled hypoallergenic soap and wash away the patchouli smell which infests my nostrils. Shampoo. Rinse. Repeat. I often wonder how many shampoo bottles I will use in a lifetime. The incessant drip continues as I turn off the shower with all of my strength. I get out into the chilly morn- ing and the drops on my body feel like water drops perspiring from an iced tea left out in the summer sun.

In the quiet of the morning, Steinbeck is scratching his fleas. I leave the bathroom and walk toward the kitchen to put on a pot of coffee. I walk past my grandmother's armoire. It is one of five pieces of furniture I kept after her death. The rolled blonde wood is so typical of the twenties. It has a warmth to it with those metal vertical handles that are longer than my hands. Ever since I was a child, I have had to use two hands to open up the drawers and the cabinet.

I walk by the armoire, touching it, and step into a puddle. "Steinbeck!" I scream. The dog runs to me. He sits at my feet.

"How could you?" I ask the dog. He looks at me with that I'm-dumber-than-a-box-of-rocks- and- I-don't-know-what-I'm-doing look.

I walk into the kitchen and put my right foot into the sink. As I squeeze out some Palmolive and massage the green liquid into my foot, I observe my callouses and rinse them off. The paper towels rest atop the counter, and I pick up the roll filled with sayings like "sharing is caring" and "love is forever" in dove blue and mauve pink and wad three or four handfuls in my hands and wipe off my feet. I throw the paper towels into the uncovered trash can and see a trail of ants dancing in and out of the trash can run around a Milky Way wrapper. Steinbeck looks at me as I walk into the armoires' room with the roll of paper towels in my hand, I bend over and pick up the urine with half of the roll of paper towels. When I fling it to a dry section, and use more towels, the warm urine hits my hand and I finish picking it up. Then I walk to the kitchen, throw out the dirty towels, put the clean roll back of the counter, and start my Palmolive bath on my hands.

While I stare at the ants in the sink on the dirty dishes, I reach over to the coffee pot, fill it with water and pour it in the machine. When the coffee machine starts to gurgle and cough, I turn on the hot water and watch the little bodies of ants drain counterclockwise in the chrome of the drain.

The coffee finishes as I watch the last ant body disappear. I fill my coffee mug and walk on into the bathroom past my armoire and warped hardwood floors. Steinbeck urinates on the floor on a regular basis. He doesn't like to pee in my grand-mother's rose garden. Her spirit may scare him out there, or it might be the thorns from the thorn bushes.

I stand in front of the mirror and clean it off with the towel from around my hair. It leaves lint residue and dog hair trailing across the looking glass. Birds cry outside the bathroom window. I take the pack of cigarettes out of my bath robe, take one out, and light it. Under the sink, I bring out a home pregnancy kit, sit on the toilet, and read the directions. So complicated, it's amazing. Getting pregnant isn't this difficult. I pee into the cup and put it in a tube back under the sink. Later on in the day, is all I think.

I look down at my cosmetic drawer. Tomas is always hound- ing me to clean it out. He says I don't need make up, that I am beautiful without it. But I find fuck me pink lipstick around his collar when I do the wash at Launderland. I will never wear cheap pink lipstick. My grandmother said my mother wore cheap pink lipstick on the day she left. I have never liked pink lipstick, cheap or otherwise.

I open my tube of brown-black waterproof mascara and apply it. My mouth hangs open as if I were singing a church hymn. Then I apply pinky-brown color to my lids, a dark rose to my cheeks, and a blood red Bordeaux to my lips. Against the paleness of my skin, I look like the walking dead. I sit on the toilet seat puffing on my cigarette. Tomas doesn't like it when I smoke in the house but he is asleep. I throw the butt in the toilet and go to get a refill on my coffee. Steinbeck follows me from room to room.

"What do you want, Steinbeck?" I ask him, as though he will answer me.

He grunts and rests his head atop his paws. I see the hot spot on his left side. It looks painful. The torn-away hair leaves the flesh exposed, capillary-like and red. I walk over to his food bowl; its empty. Steinbeck looks at me as if I understand his dog behavior. I walk over to the cabinet, and bring out the bag of dog kibble. Steinbeck dances in a circle, scratching the tile with his long fingernails. I put the bag away and the bowl down on the tile. Steinbeck licks my toes and then runs to his bowl.

I sit at the counter, staring out at the unlit garden. The sun won't be up for a couple of hours. I pour myself more coffee and walk back into the bathroom. The lights flicker with the surge of electricity when I turn on the hair dryer. Old wiring in an old house. The electricity is not grounded in this house which was built by my grandfather as a present to his first wife, Miss Abigail.

I sit on the toilet seat and reach across to the black uniform pants hanging across the wicker clothes hamper that my grandmother lugged home on the bus for me for my sixteenth birthday. She thought it was the prettiest thing. She spent that night telling me that when she was a little girl all the rich people on Los would sit on their front porches in the Indian summer heat on white wicker settees and chairs. She would walk behind her father in the heat on the day before garbage day, looking for things they could use at home. Her father, Dedo, called them new-used treasures. My grandmother had tears well up in her eyes that night at the shame she was experiencing again telling me how the rich people held up their eyes and would not look at them. It was the Depression and they thought my great-grandfather and grandmother, as a little girl, would ask for handouts. The two of them were only looking for new-used items on the street to bring home. My grandmother recalled how special the iced tea looked on those afternoons and how she had warm water to drink out of a hose someone had been kind enough to offer them on one of the side streets. The white wicker clothes hamper sits in the corner of the bathroom, ratty and gray with age, but it still works.

I step over the dog and hear Tomas talking in his sleep. He turns over and is quiet again. He'll sleep the entire day away and not even bother making the bed.

9

"Let him kill the rest of the ants," I tell Steinbeck.

Steinbeck looks at me and starts wagging his tail. It beats hard against the floor from his enthusiasm. He sits in the doorway staring up at me.

I put on the dirty trousers. As I throw on my black uniform shoes and lace them up tightly, just so I won't have to tie them again during the day. A wrinkled white blouse hangs on the back of the door. No matter how much bleach I use, I can never erase the mustard residue on the front of the blouse or the sweat stains under the arms. A slight crease can only be seen above the arms. I tuck in the blouse and put on my apron.

"Look, Steinbeck. I'm ready for work." He stares up at me and wags his tail when he hears his name used.

I step over Steinbeck. He rolls over and follows me out to the front room. In the darkness of the room, I feel around on the couch for my purse and keys. I hear them clanging as I touch the soft cushions. Outside I hear a car with a loose muffler drive past the house, and then a clunk. I look out the window and the newspaper delivery man speeds down the street with fifties tunes coming out of the only open window in a twenty- year-old import station wagon with one brake light out.

I move the curtain and press my nose against the glass to see if anyone is outside on the street. I unlatch the three dead bolts and security chain as quietly as I can. Steinbeck stands on my left foot, ready to escape the minute I open the door. I push him back and open the door. Steinbeck fights me as I hold my purse and three keys among the four fingers on my right hand, ready to fend off any attacks. I close the door with a squeak and walk swiftly to my Volkswagen Bug. I jam the key into the lock, open the door, sit down, and put the latch down. The whining sound of my engine makes two dogs down the block howl. I turn on the AM radio and listen to worthless chatter, waiting for the car to warm up. I put the car in reverse and back out of the driveway. From behind a palm tree, I think I see the shadow of a figure. I reverse a little further back, looking for my fear, but I see nothing. I drive down the street, doing the California roll at the four-way stop sign. There are no cars on the road this early in the morning.

Two

THE STARS IN THE early morning darkness blink in the mass of the sky. The noise of my Volkswagen engine roars across the narrow streets and sleeping houses of Echo Park. I look down at my gas gauge and see the line pointing to empty. I knew I would have to get gas and cigarettes before I went to work. Driving down the street in the harsh yellowed white headlights of my car, I see a black cat walking across my path. I hit my brakes and my purse and all its contents fall off the seat and spill onto the floor. I watch the cat run into a hydrangea bush and disappear. On the floor is my portable life: cash, lipstick, compact, keys, change, and shreds of dried tobacco on the rubber mat. I drive down Berkeley Avenue to the Arco station. Across the street the businesses are caged with large bars and padlocks the size of a fist. Tagging in black, silver, and burgundy decorate the old concrete walls. Names like Smiley and Mousey litter the walls and shop fronts of the carniceria, Launderland and the vacuum repair shop.

I pull into the gas station to the only available spot. The white neon lights and gas fumes fill the area above the flat black concrete. On the floor of the car, I see a ten-dollar bill. As I reach down to pick it up, a four-door sedan whizzes past and I can feel my car shake. The car rushes over to the phone booths on the far side of the station in the dark. I take my money and walk over to the cashier booth. I see the outline of a middle- aged woman on the phone. Her back is to me. Her brown hair is swept up in a French knot and it shines against the neon. Her small hands hold the receiver.

I stand in line. A tall man with a crew cut of three- quarter inch salt-and-pepper hair stands in front of the bullet proof glass. He charges his gas and asks for a pack of Life Savers, wild cherry flavored. I watch him. He looks me in the eye and walks passed me. His blue eyes and soft smile don't match his strong voice. The blue flannel plaid shirt and blue jeans he wears on his trim figure look like a uniform. I watch him walk back to his late model import sedan. He washes his windows, slowly scrubbing with the sponge and carefully guiding the rubber blade across the windshield. He wipes the excess water off with the gas station attendant's light blue paper towel. He lifts the hood of his car, and I step up to the window. The Mexican man in front of me in the line steps to the side to count his hand full of change. He stands next to me. I look at his sunburned arms and worn hands as he counts his change in Spanish.

"Five dollars on number two," I say. "Number two, five dollars," the attendant says. He doesn't look at me. He stares at the computer and punch- es the keys. The nametag on his uniform shirt says Roberto. His black hair is cut short above his collar and ears. The gold wedding band on his left-hand looks small and tight on his finger. He smiles at me. I see the gold bridge in his mouth and the gap between his two front teeth. "Five dollars' change," he says. "A pack of Marlboro Lights, please," I add. "Three-fifty," he says. I hand the five back to him. The Mexican man stands be- hind me. I listen to his heavy breathing and feel it against my neck. I take my change and put it in my pocket. As I step away from the window, I heard the Mexican man buy five dollars' worth of gasoline.

"Here," I say as I hand the Mexican man the change from my pocket.

"No, thanks," he says with pride. "It's OK," I insist. "No, Senorita," he says. The man behind the glass starts talking to the man. Three years of Spanish in high school and I can only pick up key words and phrases. The Mexican man's voice is getting louder and so is Roberto's. I hear the word 'guera'. I'm sorry for what I've done. There is no way to get out of it. The Mexican man walks away angry. I stand there and Roberto signals me to go away with the brush of his hand. As I walk back to my car, I feel the eyes of everyone on me. I'm embarrassed.

I step off of the platform and I see the Mexican man pumping his gas. There are three sets of eyes watching him. Two little girls with long braids folded up in half with ribbons and a small boy with a bowl cut stare out the window with their light brown skin and chocolate brown eyes. They look tired, but smile at the man. He makes finger puppets with his hands and they giggle with pleasure. A woman in the front seat turns around to them, and says something. They stop moving, but still continue to giggle. I look in the front seat and I see a woman close to my age with a small baby in a soft pink blanket resting against her breast. She is a modern-day Madonna in an old hatchback with dents and Bondo and a taped left rear light. The Mexican man stares at the black top as I walk by him.

In front of his car is the man with the wild cherry flavored Life Savers. I walk by his car and look in the back seat. There are work papers and books in view. He gathers up the trash in his car and throws it away. He gets in his car and zooms out of the station.

A young couple drive up in a convertible Jeep. Two surf-boards sit in the rack above the car. I stand and pump my gas in the island across from them. I watch the way he looks softly into her face and the way he brushes the hair off of her face tenderly. He smiles and whispers something into her ear. They smile and giggle, holding each other with long kisses. He touches her face with the outside of his hand and looks at me. He smiles. It is a smile I used to see.

Tomas and I had been happy. On that day in Atwater when I first set eyes on him, I thought he was too good looking for me to take seriously. We spent the entire day on the sidewalk talking about our hopes and dreams. He was an actor, working as a bouncer at a club. I thought that was so creative and wonderful. He was someone I had always wanted to meet. And now he sleeps in my bed, no longer sharing his dreams.

The pump clicks off and I top off the tank ignoring the do not top off sign. The morning begins to open, and the birds sing. I look at the indigo blue sky and I feel distanced from the world. The woman with the French twist is still on the phone. The young man from the couple pumps his gas. He walks over to the young woman. She sticks her head out of the window and he kisses her on the lips. I watch with sadness.

I put the car in neutral and start her up. The high pitch of the engine drowns out the images of the gas station. The one thing that always works in my life is this car. It was the smartest investment I ever made. Grandma would have been proud of me.

I drive up Glendale Avenue and I remember the last day. Grandma was a great woman who lived in the shadow of my grandfather's first wife, Miss Abigail. She had only one child, my father. She raised me through the memories and absences as best as she could. It was only six years ago that she died.

On the last day of my grandmother's good health, she wanted to go to McDonald's. Grandma couldn't drive anymore, so at eighty-two years old she and I climbed the mountain of Montana Street. We started out at three in the afternoon. She wore her polyester blue floral dress with the threadbare zipper in the front. Her knee-highs were rolling down her legs to just above her tennis shoes. I walked behind her, following her tight bun. She had to stop twice just to catch her breath on the way up the hill. Grandma didn't talk when she walked; she said it was pointless. In silence, we walked the streets where she had spent most of her life. When we got to the light at Alvarado and it turned green, she made me hold her hand as we crossed the street.

"Grandma, I'm a grown woman. I can cross the street on my own," I insisted on that cloudy day.

"Sage, do as I say." "But, Grandma." "We can turn around and go home, if you like. I thought it would be nice to take you out to dinner."

"Yes, ma'am," I replied. We missed one light because of our arguing.

I held my grandmother's hand as we crossed the street. Her hand was so small and fragile. The veins were thick on the sur- face of her freckle-covered hand. When we crossed the street, I tried to take my hand back. As she held my hand, we walked down the street and into the McDonald's. In line, she continued to hold my hand. She didn't ask me what I wanted, but ordered for both of us.

"A vanilla shake, and a Happy Meal, with an orange soda."

"Huh," the sleepy-eyed girl said in her blue and white striped uniform.

"A vanilla shake, a Happy Meal, and an orange soda," Grandma repeated.

"Happy Meals are for children." "A vanilla shake, and a Happy Meal with an orange soda," Grandma said with an edge in her voice and a red flare in her face.

"Ma'am, Happy Meals are for children," she said, "I mean for little kids."

"Why can't I get what I asked for?" Grandma asked. The manager

16

came to the register and whispered something in the ear of the girl.

"That's four twenty-five." Grandma paid her and I followed behind with the tray. We sat in a brown plastic booth. She stared out the window, not touching her drink.

"I thought you were hungry," I said. "I wanted to take you out for dinner. I'm not really hungry. Sagey, I'm tired. I'm not sure if I can walk back

"Do you want me to call a cab?" I asked. I always offered, but she never took me up on it.

"Maybe, but after we're finished." I looked at my grandmother and she did look tired. "How are you doing?" I asked. "How's your meal? I wanted to talk to you about something, but it can wait. I'll talk to you tomorrow," she said as she took off her glasses and rubbed her eyes, the indentations on the sides of her nose red and swollen.

We sat at the table in silence. I called a cab. He drove us home. Grandma walked straight in the house and into her bed- room. She went to sleep early that evening and abandoned her good health. A month later, I was holding her calloused and thorn-scratched hand in my hand. She was dying.

When I drive up this street, I think of her. I remember the hearse driving under the dirty gray clouds to St. Theresa's. The church on the dead-end hill overlooking downtown Los Angeles. There are days I stop by the church and light a candle for her. When I speed up Glendale Avenue, I don't have to stop at the light at St. Theresa's. If I drive slow, I have to wait for the light; and then I look over at the church and remember. This morning I am slow. I miss the green light.

I sit at the red and light up a cigarette. I watch a chrome shopping basket being wheeled across the street in the cross-walk. The cart wobbles because of one missing leg. A young man with stringy long blonde hair wheels the squeaky cart. I am the only car on the road. He wears soiled blue jeans with holes in the knee and a firehouse red polo shirt with all three buttons missing. There is a layer of dirt on his face and he smiles at me. He has no front teeth. He wheels the cart next to my car.

I look up at the light saying a silent prayer that the light will turn green so I can get out of here. The guy walks up to my car and knocks on the window. I open the wing window.

"Yeah?" "Got any spare change?" he asks.

"No," I respond. The shopping cart rests next to my right front fender. "Well, can I get a cigarette?" he asks. "Sure". I hand him a cigarette, watching the layer of filth and dirt on his young hands. He takes it between his two fingers. A wart is growing on his right index finger. He can't be more than thirty. His cloudy eyes look like the whitefish chubs at work dried out and empty. The light is still red. "Have you got a light?" he asks as he stands closer to the car.

"Sure." I hand the book of matches to him. "No, you light it," he says with anger. I throw the book of matches out the wing window, put the car in first gear and push my way through the just turned green light. The basket scrapes the fender of my car. I drive off and look in my rearview mirror. I see the chrome basket on its side in the street; the guy is standing there with the cigarette in his mouth leaning into where my car used to be and waiting for a light.

At the top of the hill, I look back. He still stands in the middle of the street. I drive down the hill picking up speed along this boulevard of sleepy apartments and Craftsmen houses. By the cobalt blue of the sky, I see the white plaster of the headless rider on the lion statue which rests atop a bluff of green grass. It was an old advertisement for The Red Lion Tavern which sits a half block away.

Another memory I have of my father is at The Red Lion. He knew the old owners, before the wife blew her head off in a selfish suicide. My father had been reading Of Mice and Men to me on our sunny front porch. He was near the end of the book with only a few pages left to read to me.

"Sagey, why don't we go get some dinner?" he asked. "Can Grandma come along?" I asked. I heard him go inside and ask her. Grandma didn't like to go out to eat; she said it was a waste of money. She said she could cook anything better than they did out. The few times we ate out, she only got a drink. Then when we would get home, she would head straight to the refrigerator to open up the butter and preserves. Grandma would eat toast. Toast was her mainstay.

I sat next to Dad in the cherry red bench seat in his old Falcon, and we drove to The Red Lion up the slight hill of Glendale Avenue. As we drove, he told me the story of the statue that Frank had bought for Marie, the owners of The Red Lion. It was her suggestion to put it up on the hill, because people would see it and think of the restaurant. Frank bought it for Marie on their first anniversary when they were both young and unwrinkled. When I walked into the restaurant, Frank greeted my father with a wave, and promptly brought over a Heineken and a shot of Wild Turkey. By then, Frank and Marie had celebrated their fortieth wedding anniversary.

In the tavern, I sat across from my father in a round booth eat- ing knockwurst and beans, and slurping my Shirley Temple. In the low light, I could make out the shadows of his face. I listened to his learned voice speak about the lives of George and Lenny. He spoke the words as if he could feel every emotion which these two characters experienced. I held my Holly Hobbie doll close to my heart as I listened to him. The husky whisper as he finished the last line gives me goose bumps even today.

"Now what the hell ya suppose is eatin' them two guys?" my father said as he looked me straight in the eye over the frame of his reading glasses.

I looked at my father while he silently mouthed the last line again. As he picked up his shot glass, his hand shook. He threw the burning liquid back in his throat, swallowed, and sat with his head bowed in his own special prayer.

The memories of my father are few and blurry. I drive down the boulevard and stop in at Winchell's. Inside I order coffee with double cream and sugar, and my twist from a woman who looks busy. Hair is falling out around her brown pony tail and she has flour on her left cheek.

"Thank you," I say, giving my order. "Have you got any chocolate donut holes?"

She walks to the back kitchen, and returns with a bag. "Half dozen, right?" "Thanks". She disappears into the kitchen and I listen to her curse at the burning donuts.

In the empty lit parking lot, I am the only car except for the lot cleaner in a loud truck which sucks up the dirt like a gigantic vacuum cleaner. I get into my car and pull back onto the streets as sunrise is on the horizon. I listen to early morn- ing talk and choose the road which drives me past the location of what used to be the hospital where my mother was born. All that is left is the ruins of a white concrete staircase with a large power pole in the shape of the pyramids in the middle of the flat ground. I feel in my pocket to make sure the postcard is still there. I can feel it. I just don't want to lose it.

The old concrete of the Victory Bridge begins to absorb the light of the sunrise as I drive past the Dutch-American Bakery. It is too early for business, so their tables and chairs are locked up inside. Yellow. Red. Green. I get stopped at every light in this exact pattern.

Down the street I drive with the twist in my mouth. I get stuck again at a red light. I feel a set of eyes staring at me in the only other car on the road. I look over at the car and a bald man with a wrinkled forehead has his mouth open and is sticking his tongue out at me and then licking his lips. He is

20

disgusting. The light turns green and off I race down the street ready to fight anyone who gets in my way. The guy turns down a side street. I head up the main boulevard filled with car lots and cars painted earth tone hues, colors other than white. I drive large city blocks, finally arriving at the street where I turn and park my car in the underground parking lot. The whiteness of the morning begins to show some signs of light.

Three

WHEN I OPEN MY car door in the darkness of the parking garage the smell of grease comes from the kitchen of the delicatessen across the street. The perfume of salted meats and stuffed cabbage dance together down this side street. I have no fear about being in the garage by myself because I'm not alone.

Delmar lives in this parking structure, at one far corner where someone punched out the light, hoping he would go away. He doesn't mind the darkness. He likes it. Delmar holds all of his worldly possessions in a chrome shopping basket. He has a newspaper clipping from a car accident he had in 1954. He fell asleep at the wheel of his cab and hit a lamppost. There is a black and white framed picture of him as a newborn baby in his mother's arms. He also has a deck of cards, a book from the Navy which holds his honorable discharge, and a couple of medals with yellowed and frayed ends folded into the pages.

I bought him a red plaid sleeping bag from the thrift store. He wouldn't accept it. He did, however, accept the navy-blue pea coat I found for him at St. Vincent's thrift store in DTLA. He said the sleeping bag was too bulky, whereas the coat was wearable. I hid my disappointment with a girlish laugh and tilted head.

I get out of my car and lock it. The bag of chocolate

sprinkled donut holes and coffee double cream and double sugar are in my hands. I go in search of Delmar. It is the breakfast of champions, the breakfast which he prefers. He is sleeping against the concrete corner. Flattened brown bags are under his feet and a light blue soiled sheet hang around his shoulders, shawl- like. His eyes flutter as a quiet whisper of noise escapes his mouth. I walk up to him, yesterday's newspaper held firmly in both his hands. I shake his right foot, slowly moving it back and forth. Delmar doesn't like any physical contact with his skin. He opens his old, salty blue eyes and looks at me.

"Morning, Sagey," he says. The Southern twang present in his speech.

"Good morning, Delmar." "What did you bring this morning?" he asks. His curiosity boils out of his body like a plastic bag filled with overcooked instant rice flailing in the water.

"What else but your favorite breakfast." "Chocolate donut holes and coffee, double cream and double sugar. Sagey, you're gonna make some man a great wife one day. Wait a minute. I'll be right back."

I watch Delmar stand up, using the cart as a crutch. He has a swinging gait as he walks over to behind the thick round concrete column. I sit kneeling on one knee as I listen to him urinate against the concrete wall. My head is turned away be-because I don't want to strip the last amount of self-respect the man has for himself. I listen to the mechanical zip of his fly as the teeth of the zipper meet. He slowly walks back over to me, wiping his hands on his dirty grey corduroys. Delmar obsessively wipes his hands on his trousers until he arrives at where I am kneeling.

"Have a seat, Sagey. You got time before going in?" He asks.

23

"Yeah, I've got time. They won't let me come over here anymore. Miss Lee said that she saw you steal a piece of lemon bundt cake yesterday. I said you would never do anything like that. Miss Lee said you aren't welcome in the deli anymore. I'm sorry, Delmar. I really am. I know you like to sit in there, read the paper, and have coffee for a couple of hours. They don't understand."

"Oh Sagey, it's not that they don't understand; they don't care. There's a big difference; its human nature," he sums up. "Fear of the untenable future."

"Maybe, Delmar, maybe," I say. The hands on my watch move slowly. The second hand seems to forever point to twelve.

Assorted cars enter the parking structure driving fast and pulling into their spaces slowly. When I look at my watch, I have only a few more minutes. I'll have to leave him out here alone and unprotected.

"Look at these people, Sagey. They don't even see me over here. I'm here day and night, and they never look at my face," he mumbles.

"Delmar, they're going to work," I answer. "They don't look at my face when I serve them food. They only look at the menu and the check. They ask me blank questions like how am I doing- ing, when they don't really want an answer. They want what they want when they want it. Less than a decade of serving has been too long."

"Don't be so negative, Sagey," Delmar lectures. He looks down at his hands, pushing his cuticles back with his half-inch fingernails.

I watch him. He is lost in his own world. Delmar sits staring at his fingers. He obsessively keeps pushing his cuticles back until they bleed. I stand up on both feet. I must go to work.

"Delmar, I have to leave," I tell him. He looks up at me with glazed eyes. Delmar's soiled face looks like an apologetic rat. I can see the faint traces of freckles under the blush of dirt. His eyes look desperate. I feel badly.

"Don't go," he whispers. His wine smeared lips barely move. "I'll be back. I'll come and visit you after work," I tell him. "No, you won't. You're like all the other cockroaches," he says angrily. Then Delmar begins to wring his hands together. His white knuckles contrasting against his red, bloody cuticles. He pushes his hands together like a lone competitor in the Santa Rosa World Championship of Arm Wrestling.

"What?" I ask. I look at Delmar and see the same expressionless face of my mother, like a Joshua Tree in the desert. She is on my mind today as the clouds roll in. I quickly move my hand to check the bulge in my pocket, the postcard is still there. Those lotus pink lips sending a kiss of automatic love and acceptance, with bits of dried skin and distended color, is still there.

"Look at these people and don't become one of them. Sagey, I refused to become one of them. I stood my ground. This little piece of concrete is mine. Nobody can take this away from me. This is all mine. This is Delmar land," he says waving his hand like a magic wand, useless the day after Halloween in the dis- count bucket.

"Don't be this way, Delmar." I was attempting to diffuse the time bomb which lives in Delmar's heart.

"Just like cockroaches when the lights turn on. Look at them. They forgo the last crumb to seek shelter from the light. Life isn't like a rat race. Rats are far too intelligent to be compared to humans. I've lived with some of the most intelligent rats. People are cockroaches, running from the light and feeding off of the crumbs that are left over," he mumbles.

I look at Delmar and feel sorry for him. He is a newborn wanting to be scooped up into the loving arms of his mother. He is lost forever in his own special world. He is 50 grit sandpaper in a world of 600 wet and dry.

"Cockroaches," he screams. He stares at the ground in his own private revolution for sanity. The holes in his soul marred by unmerciful disaster, nevermore.

I look around at the people getting out of their cars and staring at us. I think about Tomas lost in his perfect slumber in my sheets, in my bed, and in my house. I get angry, a red flash of heat begins at my face and works down to my toes.

"I'll see you later, Delmar," I say as I stand up on my two feet, awkward and doe-like to get my balance.

"Cockroaches, you'll become one of them, Sagey. Don't do it. Save your money and escape. Run away. Cockroaches. They'll get us, if you don't watch out. Step on them and kill them, all of them. You can do it. Sagey, you can do it," he mutters.

"Goodbye, Delmar." I walk away with a twist in my gut and a dream to bring home this lost puppy.

"Sagey, tell Miss Lee I loved the cake. And I'll do it again. I don't eat crumbs like the cockroaches. I want the whole piece of cake. I'll steal from her again, because I'm not a cockroach. Hee, hee," he laughs.

One hundred feet away from him, I turn around to look at him. He sits leaning against the concrete of the parking structure, pushing his cuticles back and staring down at them. He continues to laugh, denying his role as a cockroach. He looks up at me with those glazed eyes and a chill overtakes my body. As I exit the parking structure, I light up a cigarette. The sun is filtering through the clouds now, blinking against the paleness of the sky. I can hear Delmar screaming and laughing. The word crazy, as simple as it is, does not suit him. The reverberation is frightening. Anxiously I feel for the post- card in my pocket, just to make sure that I didn't lose it. The wrinkled card is still there in the factory stitched muslin of my pocket.

I step off of the curb into a street of unevenly filled pot holes. Rocks and pebbles are strewn everywhere. Their sizes range from ping pong balls to a wad of gum. Glass shards from green and brown broken beer bottles are held together by their torn white labels. The lit deli sign blinks through the dirty tinted glass windows and burgundy canopy advertising "Restaurant, Bakery, and Catering". I stand in the street, bathed in the invisible shadow of my future.

"Hey, Sage," greets Paul. He works at the camera shop up the street. Paul has to save money for bills. He gave up eating lunch and occasionally comes in the restaurant for a bagel and coffee in the morning.

I cross the street and wave at him, I hear a soft sound on the concrete. When I get to the other side, I look back and there laying in the middle of the street is my crumbled-up postcard. I run to pick it up without looking both ways. A speeding car swerves to miss me. I look at the chrome grill as it whizzes past me. "Stupid idiot" wafts out the opened car window. In that quick time frame, I think of Rose of Sharon.

It was a calm summer day on a perfect Sunday afternoon. Mom, Dad, Rose of Sharon and I were at Echo Park on a picnic. The palm fronds shivered as the wind brushed them high in the sky. The sky was blue and clear, like a bottle of antiseptic mouthwash. The air had the stale smell of burned machaca, stringy and charcoal black. Cobs of sweet corn, plump and succulent, rested atop the grills of the squatting barbeques on the grass. Mom had fried chicken covered with corn flakes; a new recipe she had found in some women's magazine. She set the table with a white paper tablecloth and held the corners down with four red bricks she found near the lake. She kept wiping off the plastic silverware with Abba Zabba white colored paper napkins. First, she wiped the spoons, then the forks, and finally the knives. Propped up against the trunk of a palm tree, Daddy was reading a book. The large brim of his straw hat shaded his face. All I could see was the gumball pink of his lips moving to the words he read in the book.

Then there was Rose of Sharon, her blue eyes sparkling in the summer sun. Their color contrasting with the ambiguous green of the duck pond. Her Dresden complexion was flushed pink like a piece of Bazooka gum from the heat of the sun. Her honey blonde braids hung low almost touching the surface of the water as we hung off the side of the lake staring at our reflections.

"Like this, stupid," said Rose of Sharon. Her sugary voice reminded me of her maturity, two years and seven months.

"Look at that flower. Can we get it?" I asked. Lying next to her, I watched every move to duplicate her. Copycat. She was a saint in my church.

"That's not a flower, dummy," she said. There was an arrogance to Rose of Sharon. I wasn't sure if it was because she was the first born or because she was Mom's favorite.

"What is it?" I asked. I listened to her every word as if it were a Sunday homily.

"It's a lotus. Hold onto me. Let me try to reach it," she said. I held her knees as they almost passed the seam of concrete holding the water. I looked at the flower. It was near perfection. The pink lotus bloom danced around large inviting green leaves. Rose of Sharon flailed her arms in the direction of the lotus.

"Can you get it, Rose of Sharon?" I asked. "Almost, hang onto my feet, forget about holding my knees," she ordered.

"Hurry up, before they see us," I said. I was always the worrier. Our mother's eyes continually scanned our activities. Crossing the street without

28

looking both ways and chocolate bars before dinner were her frequent discoveries.

"Don't worry so much, Sage," she said. "Wait, I can almost reach it."
Her knees scraped the gravel.

"What are you girls doing?" Mom screamed from the picnic table.

Her voice slapped me in the face. "Nothing," Rose of Sharon said.
"John, look at the girls," Mom yelled. "What are they doing?" he asked.
My father's face never came up from the pages. Ignoring Mom, we sat on
the edge of the lake, trying to get the perfect flower. The fuchsia pink
taunting us. Those long exquisite petals enchanting us.

"I've almost got it, Sage. Just one more try," said Rose of Sharon.
"Stop them, John!" Mom screamed. I looked up at her. She sat at the
table with her legs crossed at the knees, a paper towel in one hand and a
plastic fork in the other hand. I looked over at my father, lost in the pages
of his book, his bare feet tapping up and down on the grass to a private
melody playing in his head.

"What, honey?" Dad asked. "Look at them!" Mom screamed. "Sage
and Rose of Sharon, stop that," he said. "You're upset- ting your mother.
It's too beautiful a day to do that."

I looked up at him, his face stuck in his book. I held onto Rose of
Sharon's feet, as she made one last attempt to grab the lotus bloom.

"Hold tight to my feet, Sage, I've almost got it," she said. "Hurry up,
Rose of Sharon. Mom's gonna come down here," I said looking quickly
at Mom.

"I've got it!" she said triumphantly. She snapped the bloom off as clear
gel bled from the broken stem.

"Let me see it," I said and held out my hand. Rose of Sharon pushed
herself back from hanging over the water, the abrasive concrete scraping her
knees. She held the fuchsia pink bloom in her two hands, as if it were a
baby chick or something. We stared at the beauty of the flower.

"Bad little girls. You two are bad little girls," a Chinese woman said.
She spits the words out of her mouth. In front of us stood a woman

with her black dyed hair in a ball on the top of her head. She wore a long sleeved royal blue pajama top with embroidery and ribbon sewn frogs instead of buttons. Her head shook back and forth, a silent hum escaping her lips, as she spoke to us.

"Leave us alone," Rose of Sharon said. She put her arm around me. Our flower was in her other hand.

"You ruin nature. You ruin balance of nature. You two very bad little girls," she said. She held a shopping bag in each hand, as the words spit out of her mouth.

"Go away," said Rose of Sharon. "Leave us alone." "Yeah, go away," I said nervously. I looked in the distance at the table where Mom was still wiping the unused plastic silverware. Dad was still under the tree in his private trance reading his book.

"Go away, old woman," said Rose of Sharon. "You two girls cursed now," the old woman said. "Maybe today, maybe tomorrow, but curses can take a lifetime. Never break the stem of lotus for pleasure of self. Selfish little girls, you'll get yours."

"Leave us alone," said Rose of Sharon. "Go away or I'll get my mom."

The old woman walked away. Rose of Sharon and I looked at one another. I could see the fear in her eyes only for a minute. I was scared. I believed in superstitions like saying rabbits three times at the beginning of every month. I wouldn't step on lines or cracks either because of the fear of what might happen to Mom or Dad.

We ate our chicken legs and potato chips in silence. After each bite. Mom wiped her mouth harshly. Her lipstick and dried skin from her lips transferred to the napkin. By the end of the meal, Mom's mouth was colorless and looked sore. Dad sat at the table reading his book. Every so often he would share a line from the book that he thought was exceptionally wonderful. We finished our food, chewing with our mouths open. Mom took the Hefty plastic plates and rinsed them clean in the restroom. Dad went back to his big tree. The sun had moved and now he was in the shade.

Rose of Sharon and I played. There was no day as great as a day in *the park. That was where we had our most fun. No matter how much we played, I still thought of the old woman's words. The bad luck from the lotus was silently present. Rose of Sharon held the sweet bloom in her hand. It seemed to disappear against her soft pink flesh.*

We rolled down the hill, the city spinning. We ran across the bridge into the small island and watched the old men fishing in the lake, their buckets filled with helpless fish making useless circular laps. From the distance, I could see Dad still reading under the shady tree. Mom sat at the table folding the paper tablecloth up, recreating each fold dozens of times in her frustration. She would throw it out by the time we got home, the seams tattered and frayed. I held our red ball because Rose of Sharon held the prized lotus bloom.

An ice cream truck drove around the park in slow circles, a broken melody playing on the loud speaker. Rose of Sharon and I raced back to the table to get money from Mom. We loved to buy the chocolate flavored buried treasures, always looking for the elephant prize. I followed behind Rose of Sharon, bouncing the red ball occasionally. But it was hard to keep up with her because she was older and had longer legs. By the time I got to the table, Rose of Sharon already had the dollar in her hand. We walked up the slope of the grassy hill to the ice cream truck. Rose of Sharon and I stood behind moms and dads. They stood with their children, touching their hair and smiling at them. Rose of Sharon and I always stood alone in line at the ice cream truck. I stood bouncing the ball; she stood grasping the lotus.

"Two chocolate buried treasures, please," Rose of Sharon said. "Oh, no," I said. The bouncing ball hit the truck and went out into Echo Park Boulevard.

"You wait here, and give him the money. I'll go get the ball," said Rose of Sharon.

She always took care of me. Rose of Sharon was my guardian angel.

"One dollar," the ice cream man said. I handed him the dollar. "Thank you," I said. I picked up the two ice creams and walked behind

the ice cream truck.

Rose of Sharon was crossing the busy street with the ball in one hand and the lotus bloom in the other. She smiled at me, then dropped the flower. As she bent over to pick it up, a dark four-doored sedan hit Rose of Sharon. Her body flew up into the air. She landed just behind the trunk of the car. As she hit the concrete the ball bounced across the street in a slow-motion dribble and rolled along the gutter. Her eyes were closed and a fine line of blood trickled out of her mouth. Rose of Sharon was lying on her side holding the fuchsia pink lotus in her hands close to her mouth, like she was kissing it. A drop of blood fell on one of the petals. I kneeled down by her and watched the rolling red ball travel down the street. A police officer arrived and went to find Mom and Dad. The last time I saw Rose of Sharon she had tubes on her body and a mask over her mouth in the back of an ambulance. Mom held her lifeless body, sobbing over its still- ness. Mom held the lotus in her hands, brought it to her mouth, and kissed it. As the ambulance raced off, I made the sign of the cross. The two chocolate buried treasures melted in my hands. I sat next to my father on a park bench, watching the ice cream drip into a puddle at my feet. He read his book.

"We'll leave in a few minutes. Just let me finish this chapter," he said. I waited.

I look across to the deli, to the stone meats and cheeses decorating the outside of the building. Through the window I see the lights on and Angel slowly moving the mop. I take a deep breath before I have to walk in the door and leave the world behind.

Four

IN THE CHILLY MORNING, I knock on the front glass door to get Jo's attention. Josephine is a tiny woman with a little boy haircut short above her ears and forehead. She has the personality of Grandma in the Beverly Hillbillies. I love her to death. She is the sweetest thing. I try to make eye contact with her. Through the poorly lit doorway, Jo looks like someone on a TV screen with the mute button on. Her mouth moves furiously with silent words. I tap on the glass with the keys; Jo turns and sees me. She runs over to open the door.

"Honey, how long have you been out there?" she asks. "For over an hour," I answer, but my deadpan face doesn't fool her.

"Get out of here, you little shit," she says. Jo stands on her tip toes to mess up my hair.

"Hey, watch it with the hair," I say and walk past her. "My little Pollyanna goes to work," Jo says teasingly. She turns around and goes into the little cubby hole they call an office.

The smell of bleach invades my nostrils as I walk on the still wet floor to the cashier's cage to get my book and write the check number down in the appointed wire-bound notebook. I pocket some mints and gum on my way back to the kitchen. Angel is busy doing a sloppy mop job on the new black and white tile floor that doesn't match point to point.

"Ay, Sagita, morning," greets Angel. "Good morning, Angel." "Are you hot, Sagita?" he asks, licking his lips. "No, Angel, I am not hot." I am annoyed. I walk into the kitchen and turn on the soup burners, and coffee machines. The mechanics of the job are boring. I throw my purse on the back table and get a diet coke.

"Good morning, Rey," I say. I hold the list of opening instructions in my hand. From the back kitchen, I hear voices in conflict. I walk to the swinging door and look through the broken glass. I push open the door and stand between two voices. Freddy, the chef, is arguing with Juan, the baker. Freddy holds a soup ladle in his hand. Juan holds a stainless-steel serving spoon.

"You don't know nothing!" Freddy screams. "Stupido!" Juan screams back. They are in one another's faces. They are hitting pots and pans with their kitchen utensils.

I was in the kitchen of my grandmother's house. Grandma was at the sink scrubbing the pots and pans ferociously. Loud words escaped through the keyhole of my mother and father's bed- room. Rose of Sharon was sitting across from me at the table. I watched her as she held her head up to listen to the words.

"Mind your own business," my grandmother said. "Grandma, aren't you gonna stop it?" asked Rose of Sharon. "It's not my business," she said. I sat at the table with my coloring book. First I pressed hard against the page to make a dark brown outline of the picture. Then I filled in the picture of the dog with light strokes of my crayon.

"Grandma, stop them," demanded Rose of Sharon. "It's not my place. I'll be right back. I want to make sure the windows are closed and the curtains are drawn so the neighbors don't hear our business," she said.

Grandma walked out of the kitchen. I heard her slam the windows shut. The curtain rings rolled as she pulled them across the windows.

34

"What's wrong?" I asked. "They're doing it again. Or should I say he's doing it again," said Rose of Sharon.

"What?" I asked. "You're too young to understand," she said. "Do your coloring book, Sage."

"Rose of Sharon, why are they so loud?" I asked again. "You'll understand when you're older, Sage," she said.

Rose of Sharon leaned in the direction of the voices. Large thumps were coming from the bedroom. The voices got louder. I could hear my mother cry. Her wailing hum carried across the hardwood floors. Rose of Sharon moved her chair closer to mine and put her arm around me.

"I'm scared," I said. "You'll be all right," she said. I felt the weight of her arm around me. It was heavy against my shoulder. I looked into her face and saw her strength.

My father walked out of the bedroom and into the front room. I heard urgent whispered words between my father and grand- mother. My mother's hummed sob escaped from the bedroom.

"Put your head down," said Rose of Sharon. "What?" I asked. "Put your head down on the table," she said. "Why?" I asked. "Just do it. I'll protect you. Things will be all right," she said. I put my head on the table. My ear was against the table and my face was toward Rose of Sharon.

"That's it, Sagey," she said. "You'll be all right." I could hear my father's heavy footsteps as he walked silently through the house and into the bedroom. The door slammed shut. The voices got loud again. I couldn't make out the abstract words.

"Things will be all right," said Rose of Sharon. She caressed my hair, smoothing it out against my uneven braids.

"Rose of Sharon, what's going on?" I asked. "I'll take care of you, shush," she said.

Rose of Sharon closed my eyes with her fleshy fingers. Then she covered my ear with her soft hand. I could only hear the faint word, shush, coming from her mouth.

"I'll save you, Sagey," she said. Rose of Sharon kissed the top of my

35

head and patted my head. I fell asleep under the weight of her arm.

I felt the soft hands of Rose of Sharon on my ears.

"Pull them apart," yells Jo. Her loud voice coming from her small body.

"I need these walnuts," screams Freddy. "This is over nuts?" asks Jo. "I need them for the coffee cake. We have a special order for tomorrow," says Juan.

"I'll send one of the boys out for more nuts from the store," Jo says.

I walk out of the kitchen. I see the opening line cook behind the dish out window. I've learned my lesson about not saying hello to these guys. I'll never get my eggs and toast if I don't stroke the cooks. Rey is actually the nicest cook. We have an understanding.

"Good morning, Sage," says Rey. I look at the list that Lulu, the assistant manager, created one night when she had nothing better to do. I begin to check off the list. Somewhere on the karmic highway I must have run over a dog or something and now I have to pay. I pay with my life in this temple of doom. One day I stopped by the church to see if the priest was available to exorcize the building. I do believe this place is built on unholy ground. Anyway, the priest said that they don't exorcize buildings, just people. I thought that exorcisms of restaurants would be included in that catch- all Catholic category of mysteries of the faith.

NUMBER ONE, TURN ON SOUP HEATERS AND COFFEE MAKERS. Lulu had to begin somewhere. She earned a degree in business administration. She has never waited on a table in her life. Her father supplies Miss Lee with the lox, and she's Miss Lee's niece. Lox is a cartoon colored, oil covered, smoked fish that looks less cooked than Jell-O to me. I can live without lox, but it is the mainstay of Iggy's Deli.

"Push the lox," Miss Lee whispers, when the ends turn bright orange and become hardened. They trim off the ends so no one sees them and use them in the whipped cream cheese.

NUMBER TWO, PLACE SIX KETCHUP BOTTLES OUT AT ALL THREE STATIONS. THERE SHOULD ALSO BE A BUCKET OF LEMONS AND TWO TOWELS AT EACH OF THE THREE STATIONS. THE LEMONS SHOULD NOT BE OVERFLOWING AND THE TOWELS SHOULD BE FOLDED INTO THREE EXACT FOLDS, WITH THE NAVY-BLUE LINE RUNNING THE RIGHT EDGE OF THE TOWEL AS IT IS PLACED IN THE TOWEL BASKET.

I walk around the three stations and put out the lemons and ketchup. I try to avoid Angel. He can be a pest. I believe he got caught in some tractor equipment down in Mexico, so he repeats everything. His eyes are permanently crossed under long brown eyelashes.

"Ay, Sagita, good morning," he says. "I already said good morning, Angel, "I say.

"Are you hot, Sagita?" he asks. "No, Angel." Total exasperation. "Are you hot, Sagita?" he repeats. He touches the plump black bow holding my hair tightly behind my head.

I walk away from him. He giggles to himself. Then he mutters some obscene words in Spanish.

Number two must be finished before I go onto number three. I walk to the back kitchen, and stand over the stainless-steel sink. The odor of towels soaking in bleach runs out of the bucket as I tip it over. I turn on the hot water and watch the suds go down the drain. Steam rises from the heat and I feel my makeup melt- ing down my face. I sit on the counter watching the steam and light up a cigarette despite the fact that Lulu added my name to the "No Smoking" sign. It reads "No

Smoking, Sage." The only way she found out was because I used to flick ashes on the floor. Now I stretch across to the sink, flick the ashes, and watch them go spiraling down the drain counter-clockwise.

NUMBER THREE, CREAMERS SHOULD BE FILLED ONLY AN INCH FROM THE TOP. THEY ARE TO BE PLACED ON THE TABLES WITH THE HANDLES FACING OUT. PLEASE PUT THEM IN THE CENTER OF THE TABLE BEFORE OPENING, THEY WILL OBVIOUSLY BE MOVED DURING THE DAY BY THE BUSBOYS AND CUSTOMERS.

I put my hands in the water and can feel the hair being burned off my fingers because of the excess bleach in it. The night crew never cares how poorly a job they do, as long as they do it. I'm one of the morning bitches. I have climbed my way to the top of the pile of morning bitches. I take the towels out and fold. They do not need to be homogeneous. Let Lulu do it.

As I look above the sink and finish rinsing towels, I see a large deep brown, almost maroon cockroach. His antennae flutter as he boldly crawls in front of my face. I think of Delmar and how correct he might be about humanity. This cockroach looks like the champion, the King. He probably crawled up through the old piping. This deli has been here more than fifty years, and they have never remodeled the plumbing system.

"Hi, Tomas," I say to the cockroach. Tomas is sleeping in my sheets, in my bed, and in my house. I have to do something about this. But there are times I feel as if I am drowning. Since the death of my grandmother, I have felt incomplete, almost lost.

"Are you setting tables, or what?" Mickey, the busboy, asks. He walks into the kitchen.

"I've got time, do your own work," I snap. Mickey is pissed off at me because I didn't give him a Christmas bonus. Throughout the year the other waitresses pitch in five dollars a week and give the cooks and busboys an extra bonus. I went on strike. I voiced my opinion about the extortionist methods of the establishment, so no one asks me for any money anymore. I do suffer the consequences. I have to clean my tables in the morning, because Mickey is too busy doing his side work. But he isn't too busy to clean Matty's tables, the other morning waitress.

I like working here in the early morning before the restaurant is infected with negativity. Taking the towels out, I walk out of the kitchen.

NUMBER FOUR, PLACE SILVERWARE ON THE TABLE, KNIVES AND FORKS ONLY. PLEASE PLACE THE KNIVES FACING THE FORK ON ITS LEFT SIDE, IN AN ORDERLY MANNER.

I look out the front window and at the parking structure across the street which blocks the view. The sun appears to be coming across the grey seams of the concrete. The viewless window gives me cabin fever. Taking the knives, forks, and napkins out on the floor, I walk up and down the tables putting them out. I walk on the wet floor and leave dirty foot prints where Angel has already mopped. He sees this.

"Sorry, Angel," I say to him. "It's OK, Sagita," he says. "Sorry." I'm really not. I begin to walk away from him. "Are you hot, Sagita?" he asks. "No, Angel," I answer. "Are you hot, Sagita?" he asks again. "No," I repeat. We sound like two parrots. I walk away from him and into the kitchen.

NUMBER FIVE, TWENTY COFFEES AND TEN DECAFFEINATED COFFEES SHOULD BE PREPPED FOR THE MORNING.

I stand at the coffee dispenser and pull the lever. It feels like a slot machine in Vegas. A monkey could do this job. I feel as if a dark cloud is hanging over my head. There is a heaviness in the day, an inexplicable feeling.

Five

I FEEL IN MY pocket for the postcard. I wonder if I will see her today. My grandmother rarely spoke about my mother because she wasn't her child. My father was my grandmother's pride and joy. My mother was some woman he brought home who was pregnant with Rose of Sharon. I was the honeymoon baby. My mother was normal because that was all I knew. After Rose of Sharon got killed, Mom walked around with an apron on and a soup spoon in her hand. In the pocket of that floral apron with the sunny yellow bric-brac sewn on the pocket, she had a cotton handkerchief. She also had the dried lotus bloom in her pocket. I would see it as she brought it out in her hand, and smelled the dried flower petals. That night was the last time I saw my mother. I wrote her off as lost forever.

My mother stood over the stove in my grandmother's house. I sat at the table, playing with my coloring book and crayons. Daddy was outside reading a book on the front porch.

"When will dinner be ready, Mom?" I asked. "Soon, Sage," she said. "What kind of soup?" I asked. "Rose of Sharon's favorite, vegetable soup," she said. My mother wiped her eyes with the handkerchief. Then she returned it back to her pocket.

"I hate vegetable soup," I said. "Don't be difficult. She loves it," she said. "But, mom," I said. I looked at her with those lotus pink lips. Ever

since Rose of Sharon was killed; she wears only lotus pink lipstick. She had been forgetting things ever since Rose of Sharon died. I sat out-side my kindergarten waiting for her one day. She never showed up. Grandma came by and picked me up. Grandma and I looked at one another and never said a word about the day. That was a couple of weeks ago, Mom must have forgotten Rose of Sharon was killed running after the bouncing red ball.

"I have to go out," Mom said. She stood over the pot of soup on the stove, not looking up at me.

"But what about dinner?" I asked. "Come here, Sage," she said. "Why?" I asked. "I want you to stir the soup while I'm gone," she said.

"Mom, I'm too small to stand over the stove. And Grandma said I'm too young to be near the open flame," I said.

"I'm your mother and I say you're old enough," she said. Mom picked up the brown wooden chair and brought it to the stove. I climbed on top of the chair which gave me two feet more of height. I looked Mom in the eye. Her glazed eyes moved quickly as she spoke.

"Now take the spoon, Sage," she said. "Yes, ma'am," I said. I stood on the rickety chair which wobbled if I didn't stand with my legs apart and resting on the opposite ends. Mom stepped away from me.

"You're not doing it right, Sage," she said. "What's wrong?" I asked. "Get in there and turn the vegetables. Move them through the broth. They need to be seasoned," she said.

"Like this," I said. I planted my feet firmly on the chair and dug into the pot with the thick handled hardwood spoon.

"That a girl, you can do it," she said. Mom moved in behind me and put her arms around me. She grasped the handle of the spoon, placing her hands over mine. She hadn't come that close to me since Rose of Sharon died. Rose of Sharon was her favorite. They would make soup in this kitchen for hours. They talked as they chopped, sliced, diced, and minced. I was never invited to join them. It was their thing to do together.

"I'll be back," she said. She stepped away from me. "How long should

I stir?" I asked. "Sage, keep stirring until I get back," she said.

"Where are you going, Mom?" I asked. "I'm going to the store," she said. "Are you going to get some on those elephant ears? I love those," I said.

I hoped she would remember how much I loved them. When Rose of Sharon and I used to get them, we would break them in half and make a wish, like they were wishbones. Rose of Sharon always managed to get the bigger half; now I didn't have any- one to split them with.

When Mom went to the store, it was always an adventure. She brought us back new and unusual things. Mangos. Passion fruit. Flan. Sweet bread. My mother embraced anything new. She had a love affair with the Spanish culture. There was a statue of a dancer which rested atop her dresser. The Spanish/ Flamenco dancer was costumed in a black and red lace dress, and a which cascaded down to her feet. The dancer had come in a boxed set with my mother's favorite perfume, Maja. My mother dabbed it behind her ears and above her heart when she felt pretty.

One afternoon Rose of Sharon and I sat on the back stairs wait- ing for our mother to return from the store.

"Girls, where are you?" my mother's voiced called out through the kitchen.

"Out here," screamed Rose of Sharon. "Guess what I brought?" asked Mom. She stood on the back porch at the top of the stairs.

"A surprise," said Rose of Sharon.

Rose of Sharon owned the same sparkle in her eyes which my mother had in hers.

"Surprise?" I asked. "Yes," Mom said. Mom sat on the stairs, one step above Rose of Sharon. She opened the white bakery bag and brought out a flat and braided pastry. It was heart-shaped.

"You girls will like this," she said. "What is it?" asked Rose of Sharon. "It's an elephant ear," my mother said. "Isn't that a funny name, Sage?"

"Yes," I laughed. "Here you go. Each one of you holds a half in your

43

hand and then pull it apart. And make a wish, I always do. The two of you have to share. I didn't want to spoil your appetite," Mom said.

"Come on, Sage," ordered Rose of Sharon. "All right," I said. "Pull," said Rose of Sharon. We snapped the pastry in two. Rose of Sharon got the bigger half of the ear.

"No fair," I said. "I got the bigger half," said Rose of Sharon. "It's not fair," I said. "She's older than you, Sage. Next time you'll get the bigger half. Isn't that right, Rose of Sharon?" Mom asked.

"Of course, Mom," said Rose of Sharon. Rose of Sharon moved up one step and sat next to Mom. My mother put her arm around Rose of Sharon. I watched the two of them in their specialness. My mother held her winged arm around Rose of Sharon. I sat on the stairs quietly nibbling my half of the pastry, staring up into the sky.

"There you are," said Grandma from the back porch. I looked up at my grandmother and her large presence stand- ing above us.

"I'm out here with the girls," said Mom. "John is looking for you," Grandma said. "I'll be right there," said Mom. "Are you ruining the girl's appetite with sugar again?" asked Grandma.

"I just wanted the girls to try something new," Mom said. "You spoil them. He wants you, now," Grandma said. She walked back into the house. "All right," Mom said. Mom picked up the bag and disappeared through the door- way. She didn't sit at the dinner table that night with us. The next day I saw my mother wearing heavy makeup. Mom wore makeup around her swollen eye. I saw faint traces of purple and ash under her bloodshot eye.

"I'll get both of you one, but you can't eat them before dinner," she said.

"But Mom, don't bring anything back," I said. I remembered her blackened eye.

"Keep stirring, Sage, I'll be back," she said. "I'm going to get bread for the table."

She bent over and kissed me on the top of my head. Then she left the *kitchen still wearing her apron and in the pocket, the handkerchief full of tears.*

I stood and stirred that pot of vegetable soup until there was barely any broth, and the vegetables were burned mush at the bottom of the it. Mom never came back. The phone rang late that night, when I was in bed. I heard my father get up from his reading chair and walk over to answer it. The front door opened and shut. The car pulled out of the driveway and drove down the street. The next morning over Cream of Wheat and toast, my grandmother and father said only two things about the previous night. They said that Mom wouldn't be back and that "something happened". I wouldn't let my Grandmother throw out the pot of soup, it stayed in the refrigerator until it permeated all of the contents, and the kitchen.

Last night the newscast said it would be crystal clear. I feel the clouds gathering outside and taunting me.

NUMBER SIX, THREE POTS OF COFFEE AND ONE POT OF DECAFFEINATED COFFEE SHOULD BE MADE BEFORE OPENING. EACH OF THE THREE STATIONS SHOULD HAVE A POT OF HOT WATER AT IT.

I stand at the coffee machine and flick the switch. Miss Lee walks through the kitchen door from the deli side.

Miss Lee is a tiny woman with short hair, cut just above her shoulders, and bangs, cut just above her eyebrows, in a Chinese dyed black color. It looks like the color of undiluted India ink. She wears a professionally laundered white cook's blouse over her clothing and black nubuck one-inch heels which smack the tiles when she walks in the restaurant. Her brown and beige striped Fila purse/briefcase hangs too low on her hip, because it was made for a standard height woman. She walks up to the coffee machine with her coffee cup in her left hand and a teaspoon inside of it. The cup is already filled with cream and

45

sugar. She stands in front of the machine, and looks in my direction.

"Let me get that for you, Miss Lee," I offer. She does the same thing daily. If I'm out on the floor, she actually waits until I come back into the kitchen to pour the coffee for her.

"Yes, get the coffee for me, Sage," she commands. She looks at my wrinkled white blouse and walks with her coffee cup into the back office. She spends hours counting the money from the previous day.

One day I had to go and ask her for tape for the adding machine. I knocked on the door in the back hall. I had to knock so long my knuckles were raw and tender. She answered the door, opening it up only an inch, to see who was there. When she opened the door, she did not invite me in. I saw the pile of cash and coin on her desk. And there were all of the checks she was going through. She was making sure we charged for everything extra, no free food to anyone. No one got anything free from Miss Lee.

NUMBER SEVEN, TAKE THE BAG FILLED WITH THE PREVIOUS NIGHT'S SOFT COPIES AND PLACE THEM IN A BROWN PAPER BAG. WRITE DOWN THE DATE ON THE OUTSIDE OF THE BAG AND PLACE IT ABOVE THE MILK MACHINE. THESE WILL BE COLLECTED WEEKLY AND WE DO LOOK THROUGH THEM. THE DOORS WILL BE OPEN SHORTLY. PUT YOUR THINGS BACK IN THE LOCKER ROOM. AND REMEMBER TO SMILE, BECAUSE THIS COULD BE YOUR LAST CUSTOMER. YOU NEVER KNOW, SMILE. AND IF YOU DON'T LIKE IT, QUIT.

I take the brown bag and fill it with the soft copies. I heard they throw them out in the trash because Miss Lee doesn't like any filth or untidiness in her office.

"Hey, Rey, what is the date today?" I ask him over the dish out window.

"Vente de Diciembre," he answers. "Thanks," I say. And it all made sense. The dark clouds which visit me ever since I was a little girl, always appear today.

The day was December 20, 1968, and I was a very little girl. Daddy was reading The Pearl his black leather chair. I was playing with my dolls and the early evening turned cloudy out- side my bedroom window. I pressed my nose against the glass to look outside. The wind howled, the palm trees whispered "shush" with their graceful movements, and the orange of the harvest moon shined brightly across the shadow of my house.

Six

ON DECEMBER 20, 1968 *John Steinbeck died in New York City of heart trouble. On December 20, 1968, John Morgan closed his tear-filled eyes for a second to catch his breath. He slammed the telephone receiver down after having spoken to a co-worker. "John, did you hear the news?" the voice on the other end of the line had asked.*

"Paul, it's my day off. You know I don't watch the news or read the newspaper. Filled with the misery of other people," John said.

"Steinbeck is dead," the voice said. "Oh, no," he said. "I'm sorry, I thought you should know." "From what?" said John.

"Heart trouble." "Thanks, Paul. Goodbye," he said. I was sitting at the dining room table with my crayons, put- ting a little color into my young life. The color drained out of my father's face as he sat in the chair and began to shiver. I never noticed how small he was.

"Dad, are you going to read The Pearl to me?" I asked him. There was no answer. "Huh, Daddy?" I asked. "Maybe later, Sage. Can you bring me a blanket?" he asked. I went to the armoire and brought him the orange and brown afghan Mom had crocheted for him last Christmas. I walked up to him and he looked so tiny, shivering on the midnight black leather chair.

"Here you go, Daddy," I said. I wrapped the blanket across his body and covered his shoulders. He looked so innocent. His face was ashen, and his lips looked almost the color of a pale lotus.

"Thanks," he said. "No problem, Daddy," I said. I looked my father in the eye. He looked broken. He lifted his head up and kissed me on the top of my head. He looked so scared as he entered into his final sleep.

My father was a happy man. Despite the fact that his daughter had been killed and his wife was gone. He had his books. The books written by Steinbeck were all that he read. He worked at Pickwick Books on Hollywood Boulevard. He was a known authority on John Steinbeck. People would call him directly to ask questions and references about Steinbeck.

When my father worked as a taxi cab driver, he missed giving Steinbeck a ride by one cab. I always thought that if he had met him, his life would have been different. My father could appreciate and love someone else's words, but he lacked the ability to create his own.

On a day after Rose of Sharon died and Mom was gone, my father took me to work with him. We walked together down the two blocks to the bus stop. I stepped on the sidewalk around the lines and the cracks, because I was still fearful. We sat at the bus stop. I watched the cars and my father read Cup of Gold. My father didn't drive anymore because he said he could spend the time reading on the bus. The yellow-orange bus arrived, and we boarded the 91 to Hollywood. I sat next to the window. My father held the book in his hands and continued to read.

I looked all around me. I had never taken public transit. Grandma had a car which isolated her from the real world. It was midmorning and the sun shined a green color through the tinted windows. I smiled my baby-toothed smile. I was happy. The advertisements above were littered with graffiti.

I looked at the young girl sitting in front of me and I saw her read a glossy paged magazine with large color photos. She smelled like a rose garden. Every couple of seconds she tugged on a medium- sized gold hoop in her left ear. She opened her compact and saw me watching her. She smiled. I watched her tug the wire cord above the windows and a bell sounded off. She stood up and walked out the back door. She held it open for an older man with a newspaper under one arm and a cane in his other hand.

"Hey, man. You cheat," said a young guy. He wore a plaid jacket. He spoke to the three black guys sitting in the last bench seat at the back of the bus.

I turned around to see what they were doing. The guy in the middle had his hands-on top of a cardboard box. There were three playing cards creased in the middle, lying side by side but not touching.

"Man, I showed you how the game works, I ain't no cheater. That's the game," the guy in the middle said.

"Are you calling my brother a cheater, buddy?" the guy on my right asked. He wore a royal blue T-shirt with the Superman logo. His hair was shaved very close to his head.

"The game is rigged," the young guy said. His voice seemed to get softer as the sentence finished. The word rigged was al- most in a whisper.

"Don't be telling me you think my bros cheatin'," the third guy said. He wore a light grey sweatshirt that said Stanford, with bleach marks in the writing. He stood up, and the top of his head was only a couple of inches from the roof of the bus.

"I want my ten bucks back," said the guy in plaid. His face turned as red as his jacket.

"Man, you played the game and you lost. Thas' the way it iz," said the guy in the middle.

"Go away, little man. Don't bother us no more," the tallest guy said.

The guy in the plaid jacket pulled the cord. The bus stopped and he stomped down the back stairwell. I looked at the three guys who laughed on the last seat. The one in the middle lifted up all of the cards, and there was nothing under all three of them.

"Who's got the pea?" said the middle man. I stared at them and the Superman shirted guy opened his hand. The pea was in his large palm. All three of them looked at me. I smiled at them.

"Hi, little one," said the guy with the Superman logo. "Hi," I said.

50

My father sat next to me reading his book and didn't lift his head to see what I was doing or whom I was talking to.

"You saw the secret of the shell game. There isn't nothing under all three cards. The pea is in the other guy's hand."

I smiled. The three guys stood up and walked off of the bus. I sat straight in my chair, staring straight ahead. When my father and I got off the bus, he held his book in his hands. I stared down at the ground, looking at the names on the stars as we walked down Hollywood Boulevard. We arrived at his work, Pickwick Books. There were books everywhere. My father stood behind the counter animated. He smiled and spoke to everyone.

On that day at my father's work, I spent the day reading. I sat upstairs on the third floor in the children's section. Sitting Indian style on the hard grey carpet, I was absorbed in the books. Nancy Drew and the Hardy Boys could open doors and go places that I would never go. I looked down from the balcony. My father laughed and pointed out directions to strangers. As he smiled from a distance, I could see the light in his eyes. I fell in love with the pictures in the pop-up books and not the words. In the pictures, I could dream and escape.

My father walked me down the boulevard to Two Guys from Italy. We sat in the large picture window on tall plastic stools attached to the floor. I ate my slice of pizza and my father read his book. Then we walked to the bus stop. On the way home, my father read his book on the bus. I read my new picture book on the bus.

Those days are so long ago, I think, as I hear the heavy chain being dragged off of the front door.

"Sage, a pot of coffee for the deli, and don't forget the creamer," Jo screams from the deli.

I put a full pot of coffee and a carton of creamer up in the window.

"Thanks, baby," says Jo. I stand isolated by my thoughts, in the arena of my fears. "Baby, momma says thanks. Are you

51

OK today, kiddo?" Jo asks.

Looking out the clear tinted glass of the front doors, I feel claustrophobic and my head spins. This cannot be the end of the road. I think of my father and the happiness he had from his books. I think of my mother and her lotus pink lips. I think of Rose of Sharon and the happiness in her face when she finally snapped off the lotus bloom from its' stem. And I think of my grandmother who remained a shadowy figure to me, until the day she died five years ago.

Seven

WHEN ROSE OF SHARON died, I stood at the grave site not quite listening to the words. By her side, I watched the blush of the tea roses in the rain on her small casket. I inhaled their sweet perfume, reminded of the nectar of their reality. Everything that belonged to her was packed up in brown boxes and stored in the garage. Her name was never used again.

When my mother disappeared, my grandmother and father whispered about her. I would stand in my grandmother's rose garden and hear the anger of their words float out the kitchen window. Among the thorns, I felt safety. I would sit close to the rose bushes in the homemade compost, and let the thorns prick me. The blood would trickle down my legs, and stain the soft cotton of my clothing. It dried to a brownish color in the rays of the sun.

When my father died, the story telling stopped. My grand- mother found no beauty in words. When strangers were up- stairs eating large platters of starchy food, I sat on the bricks of an unfinished barbeque. My father had started it when he was young and had not found the words yet. I sat in the rose garden snapping off rose buds from the bushes and pulling off the petals of the helpless flowers. I kept the rose petals in my pockets and used them as bookmarks.

On the day my grandmother died, I sat in a sunny yellow vinyl chair with chrome arm rests. I held her hand as the will to live drained from her pallid face. In the sterile white of the hospital room, the forever yours red roses shocked my eyes.

"Sage, why did you do that?" she asked. "What did I do, Grandma?" I asked. She grabbed my hand. "Store bought," she said. "Grandma, I didn't have time," I said. "All your life, you've never had the time," she said sincerely. "Grandma, this isn't the place," I pleaded. "Think of me, uh," she said. Her eyes blinked rapidly. She creased the sheets in slow movements with her left hand. "Listen, Sage, I want you to be happy," she said slowly. I looked at her face. She had the face of my father. The look in her eye reminded me of my father that night I covered him with the afghan blanket.

"Grandma, save your strength," I said. I could feel the tears escaping from my eyes.

"Now, listen, I want you to think of me," she said. Her face went blank. She closed her eyes. "Grandma, Grandma," I said shaking her.

"What is it, Sage?" she asked. When she opened her eyes, she had the same irritated look on her face which was so familiar. It was the same look she al- ways had when I would ask her questions which she felt were trivial and unimportant.

"Fertilizer," she said, grasping my hand tightly. "What?" I asked exasperated. "My roses need fertilizer, stop by and see Steve at the nursery. He knows the brand I use. My roses need that special one, not the one advertised on TV," she ordered.

"I'll get it tomorrow," I said. I could feel the perspiration from her hand against mine.

"Why must you do everything tomorrow? I never taught you that," she said.

"I don't want to argue with you," I said. "Well then, don't," she said. "I'm not the one arguing," I said. "Stop by and see, Steve. He's a very nice young man. He knows what my roses like to eat. He's a very nice young man," she said. She took her hand back from me and tugged at the tube which was going into her nose.

"When I leave here, I'll go see him," I said. "That's a good girl," she said patting my hand. "I'm going to leave, you look tired," I said. "I'm not done, yet," she said with an annoyed look on her face. The beeps of the machines hooked up to her were loud. They roared against the uncomfortable silence in the room. This was the same uncomfortable silence which invaded the house when there were just the two of us.

It was the same silence when I would watch her make my bed when I was younger. I would stand behind the door and watch her through the three-inch space. She would shake my bed and a book would come out from under my pillow. She would sit on the bed and open the book. Dried rose petals would fall out from the page I was reading. She would read for a few minutes, then close the book and look around her to see if anyone was watch- ing her. She held the rose petals in her large hand. Grandma would make the bed and tenderly place the book back under the pillow. Then she would leave the room. The hardwood floors squeaked as she walked down the hallway. Her feet dug into the grooves of the wood with each step she took.

"Grandma, I'll be back," I said. "I know you'll be back, but I want you to listen to me," she ordered.

"Yes, ma'am," I said. "I want you to think of me as the last page in a book," she said.

"I don't really want to hear this, Grandma," I said. "I tried to do the best I could," she said. She wiped her eyes with a Kleenex. She took my hand and placed it between her two hands. "When there were just the two of us, I was tired. I had already raised your father. I was tired."

"I know, Grandma," I said. I tried to move my hand, but she ignored my withdrawing pressure and held my hand even tighter. "I made many mistakes. I let you do what you wanted. I spoiled you. Sage, I was so tired," she said. She wiped her eyes and continued holding my hand with her strong grip.

"We don't have to talk about this," I said.

"Yes, we do. When Rose of Sharon died, I closed my eyes. And in the blink of that moment, I could forget," she said.

"Grandma, don't do this, please," I pleaded. "I couldn't understand what your mother was going through. I didn't care. She was just some woman your father had brought home. I couldn't be nice to her. I felt she had taken your father away from me. But he'd been gone a long time by the time your mother came into my house. The good times had been so long ago, I fueled my life with select memories. His books had taken him away from me. And when I saw him speak to her, a rage overtook me," she said. She closed her eyes.

"Not now, Grandma," I said. "I was happy when she was gone. I thought I would have him back, but it didn't happen. And when your father died, I was lost. The only happiness I experienced throughout my life was through him. I made John the center of my world. I never knew the pain your mother suffered until I lost him. By then it was too late, she was gone," she said grasping my hand. "Listen to me, Sage."

"I don't want to. I don't want to hear this," I dropped her hand. "You have to listen to me. One day she may come back into your life. I saw her fall from life like a premature rose petal. I never helped. I couldn't help. I could only hurt. It was only when your father died, then I could see. But it was too late," she said. "I couldn't lose you. I couldn't let her take you away from me." A single tear streamed down her face. She caught it when it trailed next to her nose. "Timing is everything. Please remember that."

"Grandma, I have to leave. You need your rest," I said.

"Sage, I want you to be happy." She grabbed my hand tightly as she closed her eyes. When she opened her eyes, she smiled. "Be happy, find success."

"Grandma, I am happy. I'm going to school and working at the deli. I'm not going to be there forever. One day I will leave. When I finish school, I'll get a real job," I explained.

"I hope you do. You're not like the rest of them. You're young; you have an entire life to live," she said.

"Yes, Grandma," I said annoyed. "Listen you. I know you. You become happy with the way things are and you get lazy. You don't like change. You never have. You become happy with the way things are, because that's the way you've always done things. Happiness isn't something that just happens. You have to find it. Things and people can make you happy, if you give them the chance. Take the chance, don't be complacent, Sage," she said. Grandma closed her eyes for a few minutes. "Success is to find something you love doing and you're good at it. The rewards will be in your heart."

I placed her hand back on the bed. She looked so small, and peaceful. When I looked at her face, it looked like a transparent iris when the petals curl up at the end. I stood up and put the chair back in its place.

"Don't lean it against the wall, it'll scrape the paint," she said with eyes opened.

"Yes, ma'am," I said. "I thought you were asleep. I was going to leave."

"You can go, I won't bore you with my old lady chatter any-more," she said. The corners of her mouth curled up into a smile.

"Grandma, I'll be back later," I said.

"Why don't you come back tomorrow? Don't forget to stop at the nursery, and ask for Steve," she said. She wagged her finger at me.

"Yes, ma'am," I said like an eight-year-old. "And feed my roses. They need nutrition. They're helpless," she ordered.

"Yes, ma'am," I said. I began to walk out of the room. I turned around to look at her. She reminded me of dried up blackened rose petals. I walked back to the bed and leaned over her. I kissed her on the forehead and left a trace of blood red lipstick.

"Sorry," I said. I began to wipe the kiss off. "Don't be, Sage. Leave it. I was kissed by an angel," she said. She closed her eyes.

I walked to the door, and looked behind. She fell asleep un- der the heat of the bright white light with blood red lips on her forehead.

On my way home, I stopped by at the nursery for the food for the roses. Steve didn't work there anymore. In the sunshine of the afternoon, I knelt *in the rose garden feeding the roses. The phone rang upstairs in the house. Dogs howled as the afternoon sunlight was hidden by the clouds. After I finished feeding the roses, I went upstairs. The message on the machine said to call the hospital. I heard the words of her death as the clouds blocked the light through the old lace curtains.*

I buried her on a clear blue day, in the afternoon when the flowers smelled aromatic from the warmth of the day. The pale pink tea roses created a magnificent perfume in the air and the blanket they made kept her warm.

The front door of the restaurant opens up. The first customer of the day walks through the door.

Eight

"HONEY, JUST SEAT YOURSELF. The girl will be right there," Jo screams. The deli counter echoes from her voice. Her moppy blonde hair can barely be seen above the top of the counter.

I walk out on the floor and look for the customer. He is seated at a booth against the wall. I walk up to him. "Good morning, would you like coffee?" I ask. "Yes, and a menu." He looks down at his paper with tortoise framed bifocals stuck on the knot in his nose.

I walk to the station and fill a coffee cup. As I walk back to the table, the menu is in my hand.

"Decaf, right?" he adds. "No, it's regular. You didn't say anything about decaf," I say defending my action.

I hand him the menu and walk back to the station. Pouring the coffee back into the pot, I spill the brown liquid across the shelf. I use a stack of paper napkins to pick it up and return to the table.

"Decaf, right? I can't drink the leaded stuff. You got bacon and eggs here?" he says reading the sports section of the paper, not looking at the menu or me.

"I'll let you read the menu and I'll come back in a few minutes," I say. My body is already walking away from the table as the words roll out of my mouth.

"No, I know what I want. I've got a plane to catch, so I've got to order now. Have you got bacon and eggs?" he asks. "Yes," I say. "Then you're not a kosher deli. A kosher deli wouldn't have bacon," he says accusingly.

"We don't advertise as a kosher deli. We say we are a kosher style deli. For true kosher, you'd have to go to the west side or the valley," I snap.

"Give me bacon extra crispy and dippy eggs," he orders. He turns the page of the newspaper.

"Excuse me sir, dippy eggs? I don't know what those are," I retort. The smirk on my lips is hidden.

"What are you, a new waitress? Dippy eggs. Eggs I can dip the bread in. You must be new, I come here all the time and I don't have any trouble. Just give them to me scram- bled then. Make them scrambled easy, with onions," he says disgusted.

"What kind of toast? We have white, wheat, rye, sourdough, egg bread and pumpernickel," I say annoyingly.

"Give me challah. You do know what that is, don't you?" "Yes sir. I may be a Catholic girl working in a deli, but I know what it is," I snarled.

I walk away from the table, turning just as he was opening his mouth to say something else.

"Butter on the side," he yells in my direction. I continue walking. Rey looks at me. I hang the tag. "Sage, you take an order? We have ten minutes before open- ing. I haven't got hash browns on the grill yet. Why you do that?" he says from in front of the empty grill.

"Look, Rey. Today isn't the day. Don't push me today. Julio opened the door and the guy walked in. Then don't make it for ten minutes. I don't give a damn," I scream. I look him in the eye, ready for confrontation.

"Ha, ha," he laughs. Rey walks along the long corridor which link the deli counter to the kitchen.

I know he's going to snitch on me to Jo. But I can't help myself. I love to hear his pronunciation of her name.

"Sage, baby," Jo calls out. She appears in the window. "Baby, are you taking orders already? Honey, we don't open up for a few more minutes. Why'd you do that?" she asks winking her eye at me.

"Sorry, Jo. It's just that the guy has to catch a plane. And I didn't want him to go up to Dupar's for breakfast. You know how slow it's been. Every customer counts," I reply.

"Wait a couple of minutes, Rey. Then make it when you've got cooked potatoes. Is everyone happy now? My work is never done," she mumbles walking the line back to the deli. "Don't bother me again. I've got caterings to get out."

I walk back out on the floor. The customer is up at the station pouring himself coffee. As I get to the station I see him putting the regular coffee pot down. Let him get the jitters, I think. That will set him straight. There is a ding sound coming out of the kitchen. Rey is doing it again. When he wants to be a pest, he smacks the heat lights with the blade of a knife. It is a rather annoying sound. I walk back to the kitchen.

"All right, I heard. Don't do it again." I pick up the plate by the lettuce and beet garnish side, the cool side. I pick up the toast and plop a Smucker's grape jelly and mixed fruit jelly on the toast plate with three butters. Two is too few and four are too many. "Thanks," I mutter as I leave the kitchen with the food. I always throw a customary "thanks" in when I pick up my food. It's a habit.

"It's about time," the customer barks. I put the plate in front of him. I place it on top of the newspaper.

"Sorry," I say. "The cook wasn't ready yet." "I need

61

ketchup, and Tabasco." "Anything else?" I ask. I return from the station with the ketchup and Tabasco.

"More decaf." "Yes, sir," I say walking to the station. "Here we go," I say returning and pouring the decaf.

The customer's eyes look up when I pour the coffee. The handle I carry is orange. The coffee he poured from was a brown handle. He looks me in the eye. I put his check on the table and walk away.

"Good morning, Sage," Matty says. She walks in before her shift begins.

"How are your feet today?" I ask. "I soaked them all weekend long. I had to go to the doctor on Friday. She drained them. They feel better than they have for a long time. Damn pus pockets," she whines. She pours a cup of coffee.

Matty sits at the back table. Rey brings out a breakfast of bacon and eggs to her. She eats her breakfast in less than five minutes. Then she washes it down with a diet chocolate shake. I stand at the front station watching the clock and watching Matty drink her fourth cup of coffee.

"Sage, you got time," Jo screams across the dining room. "No," I answer. I walk over to the deli counter and lean up against the cold chrome of the case. The dried golden chubs smile through cloudy eyes. Creamed herring and green tomatoes sit on the bottom shelf, next to the plastic bags filled with barbequed cod. The oily sheen of the lox glares against the just cleaned and streaked window glass. Blood from the roast beef drips into a small stainless steel pan at the bottom of the case. The two cases filled with red meats and cheeses are clouded with condensation. All that can be seen are the tips of tongues, stiff and dried out. On the counter is Russian coffee cake baked last Thursday, but still sold for the fresh price of two dollars and ninety-eight cents a pound. On the back wall the chrome trays hold Jewish rye with the corn meal on the outside falling off at the touch of a bare hand. The undersized loaves of pumper- nickel share the shelf with the rounded, beautiful of the loaves of challah.

"Isn't she on yet?" Jo pleads.

"Let me see," I reply and lean over to see the employee table. "She must have gone to the locker room to put her stuff away. As soon as she comes out, I'll come and get you."

"You better. I need a cigarette; Miss Lee has been bitching all morning long. She said I didn't order enough bagels. I'm not the one who did the ordering. Pete did. Let her chew his ass when he gets in here. Two goddamned days of fishing and he needed an extra day off to rest. What a poor excuse for a manager," Jo says in one breath.

I walk back to the station, and bring my customer more decaf. "No, that's enough," he says. I pour more into the cup. I walk back to the station. Matty stands at the wall in front of the adding machine, taping up the schedule for today. Matty used to be head waitress until they demoted her. Now we don't have one. I wouldn't have stayed around, pride or something like that.

"I'm the front, you're the back," she says exercising imagined authority.

"I already took him. He's done anyway," I reply. I purposely sat him up on her side. It's a waitress's trick to fill the other girl's station and leave yours empty. So that when the other waitress gets on the floor, you can put all the new customers on your station. We have to seat people. The hostess doesn't come in until eleven.

"Yeah, OK," she says. "Psst," Jo whispers from the back-coffee machine. Jo pours coffee in her cup and walks over to me.

63

"Morning, Jo," Matty obligingly says.

"Good morning, Matty. Didn't I already say that to you? Well anyway, can Sage come out and play with me?" Jo asks. She puts her arm around me.

"I don't care," Matty says nonchalantly. "I'll be back in five minutes. Thanks, Matty," I say. "Come on, baby," Jo says pushing me with her one free hand. "Wait," I say and stop at the fountain for a Diet Coke. "That stuff will kill you," Jo lectures pointing her finger at the glass.

"And your coffee and cigarette diet won't kill you, eh?" I reply. Jo pushes me through the swinging door of the back kitchen. I walk by large containers of cut carrots and broccoli, and the lingering odors of salt, sugar, and oil.

"Morning, Miss," Freddy the chef, says. "Good morning, Freddy," I say. I walk through the narrow kitchen filled with half a dozen Mexican men prepping food. Freddy stands over the six-burner stove plopping uncooked matzo balls into oil slicked hot water, and watching them expand. Angel stands in front of a four-foot-wide aluminum bowl, mixing the potato salad with his hands. I see the potato salad smeared against the black hairs on his upper arms, and it stains the sleeves of his shirt. Jo pushes me up the stairs, past the jars of marinated artichoke hearts and cherry peppers. I touch a plastic jug on the shelf, and a dark orange syrupy liquid comes off on my hands.

"Nice going, Sage," Jo laughs. "What is it?" I ask. "Food coloring, girl. How else do you think they get that yellow color in the chicken broth," she says continuing to laugh up the stairs. "You didn't think they boiled down a hundred chickens just for the broth, did you?"

I open up the old seamed steel door with the "Abre la puerta," sign Freddy made. I push open the screen door with the broken hinge. Under the plastic green tarp, the catering comes alive. Jo and I stand off to one side, near the back wall and ashtray.

"Got a light, honey?" Jo asks. "Here you go," I say and hand her a book of matches. "Now tell Momma. What's bothering my little girl?" she asks. She messes up my hair with her free hand. She keeps her hand resting on my left shoulder.

Under the green tarp, I can't see the sky. It is blocked by the imitation roof.

"Jo, are you happy?" I ask. "Is it Tomas, again?" she asks. "Yes, and no," I state. "Is this the end of the line? This is my life. I always thought that when I grew up, I could be whatever I wanted to be. But Jo, I am grown up."

"Baby, I have no answers. You can leave here anytime you want. The rest of these women can't. They're professional waitresses," she answers.

"I know," I reply. "And it is about, Tomas." "Honey, you know I'm no good when it comes to advice about men. I've had five husbands and they're all planted. I guess I'm just a hopeless romantic or else I'm just a very stupid woman. I haven't made up my mind yet. No one ever takes my advice. I've told you that before." She takes a long drag off of her cigarette. "I told Pauly, that bar would be the death of him. He was worried about my health, kept telling me to stop smoking and drinking coffee. I planted the bastard six months later. He was the only one I truly loved. Pauly would give me the world. Then he turned around and had a heart attack in the wine cellar at Emilio's." She takes another hit off of her cigarette and gets lost.

Nine

STANDING ON THE OLD concrete and feeling the pebbles under my feet, I look around. I watch the kosher pickles being sliced by hand. Each cut grooving deeper into the wood of the cut- ting table with the wobbly legs. I crush out the cigarette with my fingers hard in the ashtray, mangling it among the white, black, and gray. I look around at all the men who have worked here for a hundred years. I am not one of them. I can't be.

Stepping down the stairs, I see a lower torso sticking out from the grease trap on the ground. A man next to him squats with a bucket, towel, and flashlight. They are working on clean- ing out the grease trap. The smell of grease rises above the kitchen.

"Good morning, miss," says Freddy.

"Morning," I reply. "You didn't get much sleep last night, now did you?" he asks and grins.

"How's your wife?" I ask reminding him of his status. Freddy, the chef, lives in the San Fernando Valley in a big house. I've only seen the pictures of his smiling wife and three kids. They're all grown. She has cancer. He loves her. He hasn't had sex in five years. I am always in awe of people who can love a lifetime.

"You got me, kid. I thought I could get that one by you," he acknowledges.

"What are you making?" I ask walking over to the burners. Aluminum pots three feet tall boil on the stove. I look into one, standing on my tip toes. Celery, onion and assorted other vegetables boil into transparency in the chicken broth.

"Late night, eh?" he asks grinning. "Why don't you leave the vegetables in it? It looks more like homemade with all of the vegetables. It looks almost pretty."

"Miss Lee wants a clear broth. She doesn't want anything in it, except for turkey. She wants it all strained."

"Sweet and sour soup today?" I ask. "You got it, kiddo. I'll bet you look really good with your hair down. That long hair must be so smooth to the touch. You look really good today," he says. "I could eat you up."

I have seen that man-eating look before. But it's been so long.

Tomas and I had been going out for four months. I had passed the thirteenth week which always seems so unlucky to me. One plus a dozen just seems to bottom out in my relationships. I had always accepted that as the way I was made. I went home sick after lunch. This was after the room had spun and I had dropped a pastrami sandwich in a man's lap. He was good natured about the incident, but Miss Lee didn't want to risk more dry cleaning bills.

I drove home during the afternoon traffic, opened the door to the house, and sank into the big black leather chair. Through the lace curtains, I watched the night fall. Waking up to the sound of a pounding fist, I walked to the front door. It was Tomas.

"Baby Bear, why didn't you call me?" he asked. "When I called your work, they said you'd gone home." He walked in the door and gave me a hug with those magnificent arms.

"I was going to call you later," I said. "I know what you need, Baby

Bear. You need to be taken care of, and that's what I'm going to do. I'll take care of you," he said.

"I just need to sleep," I said. I sank into the chair. "You stay right here and I'll be back," he said. "I got stuff for you."

I stare into the blue light of the old television. The colors are so gray. I put it on black and white. It's less offensive, and be- sides those are true colors.

Tomas walked in the door wearing his dashing black beret and carrying two grocery bags. I recognized carrot greens stick- ing out of a bag and celery stalks. I watched him walk into the kitchen, as I put my head in my lap.

"No wonder you're sick. You've got nothing in this refrigerator to eat. Do you know you have the pizza we had out two weeks ago in here? This is disgusting," Tomas said.

"Sorry," I whined. He walked out of the kitchen. Standing on the floor heater separating the living room from the dining room, he looked like a giant. His tight fitting white T-shirt and blue jeans accentuated his large football player's frame.

"Baby, let me take you into the bedroom," he said. "No, I don't want to go in there. I want to stay here, with you," I said. "I'll be quiet, and just finish reading this chapter."

"Sage, why do you resist me?" he asked. "Why do you need to read? You're sick. You'll never win, don't try to resist."

Tomas touched my hair with his hand. He kept caressing my hair with his soft hands. I tilted my head in his direction, absorbed in his tenderness.

"What are you going to make?" I asked. "My, aren't we the snoopy one? What makes you think I'm going to make anything?" he asked.

"Because you are, I can tell," I said. I looked into his black eyes. "What are you gonna make?" I asked.

"Baby Bear, I'm gonna make you soup. That's what you need in life, soup. I think that soup should be on the table in every home in America," he said seriously.

"But Tomas, it is. Haven't you seen all of those Campbell's commercials? Soup is everywhere," I said. I moved my head against his hand.

"Aren't we the smart little bear?" he asked. "Don't stop, I liked that," I said.

"Well, we can't always get what we want, now can we?" he said. He stood up and walked into the kitchen.

I sat in the chair listening to the kitchen. Pots and pans banged against the insides of the cupboards. The silverware drawer sounded like it was being assaulted by an impatient hand. The plastic of the vegetable bin crisper wailed.

"Have you got a big pot, Sage?" he yelled. "I'm not sure," I said. "Look in the oven. That's probably where she left it."

"Yeah, here it is. Are you gonna go to sleep?" he yelled from the kitchen.

"No, I can help you," I said. I walked into the kitchen. Tomas stood at the kitchen sink. I looked at the small tin measuring cup in his hand. He counted silently mouthing out the number of cups of water he poured into the pot.

"What kind of soup?" I asked. "Vegetable soup. That's Dr. Tomas' remedy. All you need are some vegetables and someone to take care of you. Leave it all to me. I know what you need. Some of my soup, it's magical," he said.

"I don't feel like vegetable soup," I said. I haven't had vegetable soup since the day my mother left. I hated the sight of the dark liquid with all of those vegetables, slimy and floating. Even the smell of it made me sick.

"Don't be superstitious. I'm not going anywhere, Sage. Don't be scared," he said. He walked up to me and kissed me on the top of my head.

I sat at the round Danish kitchen table. The sounds of children laughing and counting numbers outside in the street floated through the window. The old table pad was still hard under my sweaty hands. I traced

69

the white vinyl tablecloth with the trailing vine pattern, feeling the ridges of the design under my fingertips. Tomas stood with his back to me. I watched his arms move in controlled precision, flailing about the kitchen.

"Why don't you go to sleep? You'll feel better if you rest, Sage," he said.

"But I don't want to, Tomas. I'm not really that sick. Aren't you afraid you'll pick this thing up from me anyway?" I asked.

"I'm immortal, nothing can stop me," he declared. He turned around and walked up to me. Tomas placed his hand on my forehead. "You feel hot. And I can see it in your eyes. Baby Bear. You should go into the bedroom and rest."

"I want to stay here and watch you make the soup," I said. "You get to do what you want, Baby Bear. You look very cute today, did I tell you that yet?" he asked.

I watched him from a distance. If it hadn't been for that siren, his choice of reading material, and my making the sign of the cross, we might have never met. He stood in front of me moving the plastic produce bags around on the counter. "Can I help you?" I asked. I sat in the chair. "Can you cook? I had to throw that one in there, Sage." His body moved as he chuckled. "Baby Bear, I know you don't cook. Just sit there and look cute. I'll do everything."

"I can help," I said. I stood up and walked over to him. I looked over his shoulder as I hugged his backside. He felt so warm and soft. As I put my head in the crook of his back, I could smell the sweet perfume of his body.

"What are you doing?" he asked.

"Nothing," I said. I inhaled his scent. "Why don't you stand right here? You can help me. It'll be fun. Why don't you take all the vegetables out of their bags," he said? He moved away from me.

"Sure," I said. I stood at the counter by his side. When I leaned into it, I could feel the chill of the tiles under the fabric of my blouse. I lifted up my blouse and put my stomach against the coolness of the tiles.

"What are you doing?" he asked. "Nothing," I said childlike. "Sage, what are you doing?" he insisted. "I'm just cooling my body. It feels good against the tiles of the counter, that's all. No big crime, you know," I muttered.

"I know you, Baby Bear," he said. "I can tell when you're up to something. It's written all over your face. And it's in your eyes, that look."

"What look are you referring to, sir?" I said playfully. "The look you have," he said. "I don't know what you're talking about," I replied. "When I first saw you on the sidewalk that day, you had that look in your eyes," he said. "I don't know how exactly to describe it, but I know the look. It's always the same, the look in your eyes. It's when your eyes sparkle."

"Tomas, what does the look say?" I asked. "Save me," he replied. Tomas had a serious look on his face. "I know that look. I've seen that look before. All women have that look in their eyes, at least once in a lifetime. It was what attracted me to you."

"I don't think so," I said. I stood at the counter putting all of the vegetables together in one pile.

"Keep them separated," he ordered. He walked over to the cutlery drawer and opened it up. "Where are the sharp knives?" "Not in that drawer, the one on the left," I said as I pointed with a carrot. "Why did you get the carrots with the tops on them? I've never bought these before. I always think they're too expensive, especially since you throw the tops out."

"I don't throw them out. I mince the tops and put them in the soup." He opened the drawer. "I don't see it," he said.

"It's right there," I said. I moved him out of my way. "In the cardboard blade saver. That's where she always kept it." I handed him the long knife with the cardboard cover still on the blade.

"Why keep it in a different drawer?" he asked. "Oh, Tomas, don't you know anything about fine cutlery? You want to protect it, so it doesn't get ruined. Grandma always said to keep it in there and I just do it," I said. I stood in front of the cutting board organizing the vegetables. Long

71

orange car- rots hung off of the board with their greens touching me. Small red potatoes sat next to the squashes, zucchini, starburst, and crook neck.

"Keep them organized, babe. It's all in the timing," he said. "Is that in order to save them?" I asked. "Don't act like a brat, Sage. It's not very lady like." He stood in front of the potatoes and cut them first in half, and then he quartered them. "I know you're not feeling well, so I'm going to let it go."

"Tomas, what did you mean when you said that save me look?" I asked. I brushed the hair off of my face and looked at him. While cutting the vegetables, he appeared immune to my voice. "I'm just interested to hear what you meant?"

"On the sidewalk, in the blinding sun of the day, that's what the look on your face said to me. That's all I meant. Sage, it's no big thing. Can you put these in the pot?" he said. He pointed to the quartered potatoes.

"Tomas, I don't understand your logic," I said. "What does the save me look mean? I was reading and enjoying my break- fast on my day off. How in the world did you come up with your conclusion?"

"I was wrong, then," he said. The sharp blade cut through the dark green zucchini skin. He made quarter inch cuts.

"What does the save me look mean, Tomas?" I asked. I felt my brow wrinkle with misunderstanding.

"Sage, I don't think this is the time or place for this conversation. Put these in the pot, will you?" he asked. "You just don't feel well, Baby Bear." He placed his arm around my shoulder and still held the knife in his hand.

"Just explain it to me," I said. I felt a warm flush come to my face. I looked at the shiny blade in his hand. My grandmother's prized Sheffield. It still looked new. She cared for that blade with an extreme sense of pride.

"If you insist, Sage. But you realize you may not like what I have to say," he said. "Put these in, will you?" With the blade of the knife, he moved the zucchini over to me. He picked up the crook neck squash. Tomas began to slice them into half inch slices against the curve of the squash. *"What else have we got, hand me that onion. You can put these in,"* he said. He pointed to the squash.

"You're not gonna tell me, are you?" I asked. *"Calm down. I'll give you my theory on women."* Tomas took the purple Bermuda onion in his hand and cut off the two ends. He peeled the dried paper skin off of the outside of the onion. Purple skin flakes stuck to his hands.

I watched him wipe the purple liquid on the hand towel and throw it carelessly on the counter. The bluish-red tint soiled the purity of the blue and white stripes.

"Tomas, what did you mean when you said I had that look on my face which meant save me? I don't remember thinking that when I saw you." I leaned against the counter, away from Tomas. *"Baby Bear, in my experience there are two types of women. There are those women who save, and those who want to be saved. You obviously fell into one of those categories,"* he said absolutely.

"I see. I see," I said. *"On that day with the sun shining high, you looked absolutely beautiful. Sitting on the sidewalk, with the wind blowing your dress at the hem, I fell for you. The weight of the material never allowed me even to see your ankles. You were so beautiful. And with the cars whizzing by you less than ten feet away, you showed no fear. I'd been watching you all afternoon. I first spot- ted you in the thrift store a couple of doors up from the bakery. You caught my eye. The way you traveled around the shop. You were standing at the racks of clothing. I saw you quickly thumb through the hangers until you saw something which caught your eye. Then you lifted it up, against your body, and closed your eyes for a moment. That was when I could get a really good look at you. Under the dimness of the burnt out fluorescent bulbs, I wanted to talk to you. But you looked like you were on a mission,"* he said.

"I didn't see you there, Tomas," I said surprised. When I shop in the thrift stores, it's my therapy. It relaxes me to look and touch things that have a history. It's a comfort zone to me. My grandmother and I used to go shopping in the thrift stores. It was a way to keep her close to me. I was

in my own private world. "You weren't going to see anyone. You were unapproachable. I watched you walk over to the books. Every time you walked past someone, you said excuse me in a soft whisper. You were so sweet looking. As you walked up and down the aisle of books, you dragged your finger against the spines. And with those naturally pink succulent lips," he touched my lips with his big hand. "I watched you mouth out the titles of books," he said.

"I didn't see you there," I said again. "And then I saw you pull a book out of the shelf. I couldn't see the title. I was in the next aisle. I heard you quietly read the words to yourself, oblivious to those around you." He stood at the cutting board as he sliced the purple onion with small, precise strokes.

"The Grapes of Wrath," I said. "I already had a copy, my father's copy." The book is filled with his notes and doodles. My father doodled romantic vines, trailing the length of the pages of the book. All of his books have these vines trailing the pages, only now they are yellowed with age. The vines have leaves only, no flowers, buds or roses. They run the length of the page, with no beginning and no end.

"You closed the book, and put it back of the shelf. The cashier was looking at me because I had been in kitchen gadgets, just looking at you. When you put the book back, you wiped your eyes. We were face to face when you walked into my aisle. I saw the tear streaks under your eyes; they looked like cat's eyes. I moved out of your way, holding onto a hot air popcorn machine. Then I walked over to the aisle and picked out the book. The Grapes of Wrath and I opened it up. There in the title page was a still wet tear in the name, John," he said. He sliced through the heart of the onion and the sour perfume infested the kitchen. "I already had a copy of the book," I said. "I didn't want to deny someone else the pleasure of Steinbeck's words."

"When I looked around for you, you were at the glass cases. I watched you squat down and look, no, you stared at the cases," he said.

"The bell collection, someone had given away their bell collection. I remember thinking how sad they must have been, giving away the bells that made them so happy," I said. I was immune to the strength of the onion perfume.

"You asked the cashier to bring out three bells," he said. "I re- member staring at you, the cashier looked at me as I watched you." "I couldn't break up the collection. There was one bell. It was ceramic ivory white. It had Niagara Falls, 1946, written on it. It made a sharp pitch as I shook it," I said.

"I know, I watched you shake the bell. The cashier got impatient with you, and walked away. She rolled her eyes as she walked away. I watched you with The Grapes of Wrath in my hands," he said. He stood with the knife blade rested against the cutting board, and only half of the onion cut.

"There was a crystal bell, I thought it was Waterford. It had a chip on the side seam. Every time I shook it, the clear bead seemed to find its way to the chip. I was afraid it was going to shatter, but it was beautiful," I said. I lifted up my shirt again and rested my stomach against the cool tile.

"How are you feeling, Baby Bear?" he asked. "And the third bell," I said. I ignored his question. "I remember the third bell, because it almost sold me. It was a wind chime, made out of a dark brown tarnished copper, I believe. It had the most beautiful low pitch. And on the bead, there hung a turquoise and white piece of paper. There were Chinese characters written on the piece of paper, but the paper had been torn. It was missing the bottom half, which would hang below the bottom of the bell. But I remember I really liked that one."

"I know, I watched you have a silent argument with yourself. And then you delicately placed the bell back on the counter, and walked out of the door. I watched you look to the right, then left, and then right again. You walked down the street making tiny steps, and staring up at the sky," he said.

"I don't remember doing that. I don't think that's true," I said. "What was I looking for, the sky to fall in?"

75

"I remember waiting in line behind this fat woman who had to count the change out of her little old lady's coin purse. I stood in that line wondering if I could catch you. But I had to have that book filled with your tear. That was all that mattered to me," he said. He chopped up the rest of the onion.

"But you haven't explained the save me look," I said irritated. "I paid for the book, and then I panicked as I pushed my way out of the door, past other people bringing in donations. I didn't look at their faces, because I wanted to see you again. And there you were, putting coins into a parking meter. You were hitting the meter, because it wasn't registering the coins you put into it. You were rocking that meter with both hands, until it would comply with you. I stood in the doorway of the thrift shop laughing at your perseverance. Baby Bear, you had such a determined look on your face." The purple onion juice poured soupy on the counter. Tomas wiped it up with the pink and white celluloid sponge.

"Explain the save me look," I said. I was losing my patience. Tomas had a habit of dragging everything out.

"I waited until you came out of the bakery. I watched you from the doorway. I thought you saw me staring at you and then I had to get out of the way of a king-sized mattress and bed frame. But you didn't see anything. You were sitting down at a table, and then you brought out your book. Every time you took a bite of that honey pecan sweet roll, you wiped away the crumbs with a paper napkin. And you read Cannery Row, so intently. It wasn't until I saw you make the sign of the cross that I knew you saw me," he said. Tomas was lost in his memories.

"Save me?" I huffed. "There are two types of women," he said. He poured the onion in the pot. "Have you got any garlic?" he asked.

"In the drawer where you got the knife, it's in a paper bag," I said.

"You keep your garlic in a drawer? That's a weird place to keep it," he said.

"That's where Grandma kept it, and that's where I keep it. I don't use it. It's really old. That garlic has been in there a long time," I

76

explained.

"*Garlic keeps,*" *he said. He brought out a paper bag, and took out the head of garlic. "It has some soft spots, but I can cut them off. It's mostly for flavor, and to kill that bug you've got. Garlic is the flower of good health. You should eat more of it.*"

"*Yes, sir,*" *I said. "So, there are two types of women,*" *he continued. He peeled the skin off of the cloves and placed seven cloves into the soup. "There is the type which save you and want to change you. They feel that they have the one secret which will make you whole. And they spend all of their time trying to convince you that they are the only one with the key. These women make men their projects, like baking a cake. All of our qualities are like the ingredients on a kitchen counter when you're making a cake from scratch. They think they can change the recipe, but these women don't think.*" *He placed the top on the pot of soup. He turned around and stood directly in front of me. "They don't think that by altering the recipe, you change the end product. And that my dear, Baby Bear, is the horrible saving type of woman.*"

"*But they mean well, Tomas,*" *I added. "It's not that easy. Life isn't so strict. There is a lot of give and take. It isn't just black and white.*"

"*You, my dear, are not that type. Baby Bear, you don't have to worry. You are the type of woman who needs to be saved.*" *He ran his hand down my right side, caressing it with his big hands.*

"*That's stupid,*" *I said. I moved away from him. "When I looked in your eyes on that day, and you made the sign of the cross, you were so innocent. Like a child, you turned around to see if anyone had seen you. You were so cute. I re- phrase that, you are so cute,*" *he said. He walked up to me and hugged me.*

In his arms, I felt like a puppet. I was wordless.

That night, I sat up in bed and he sat next to me. Under the naked bulb of the overhead bedroom light, he fed me vegetable soup. I chewed every mouthful and smiled at the small spoon in his big hand.

In the lucidity of the broth, I am brought back to the kitchen at work.

"Hey, girlie, are you listening to me?" Freddy asks. "What?" "They're calling you out front, Missy, I think they need you out on the floor," he says.

"Oh, thanks," I say. I walk on the one-inch rubber mats, grasping onto the slippery floor with my small steps. I push open the white laminate swinging door, and don't look through the cracked diamond glass, the looking glass.

Ten

"I NEED YOU ON the floor, what are you doing back there?" Matty asks.

"Just taking a cigarette break," I reply. "Day dreaming, and socializing are more like it," she replies. She pushes past me with two coffee cups balanced in her left hand.

"What's her problem?" I ask Rey. "I don't know," he says shrugging his shoulders. I know what her problem is, it's always been the same. Matty is a professional waitress. She was born to do this job. It's in her blood and her dyed copper red hair that is wedged on the crown and shaved short along the hair line. Her thick Pillsbury-doughboy arms dangle at her sides with those coral orange silk-wrapped fingernails. Hazel eyes sit under penciled in reddish-brown eyebrows. Lips in the same coral orange make her look like Ronald McDonald. If I'm sick, she's sicker. If I'm ill, she's dying.

"Sage, you've got customers waiting on table six. They've been there a long time," Matty growls. She pours one cup of coffee and walks out on the floor.

It was Lulu's idea to number the tables. I know where each table is, I don't need numbers. Lulu has a master plan for the restaurant. She should remember it's a delicatessen, and not a restaurant. People don't mind if you slap their sandwich down in front of them on a plastic plate. In fine dining, you cross serve, you never put your elbow in someone's face. Here, they inhale the sandwiches so quick, it doesn't matter what they look like. In the blink of an eye, the sandwich is gone.

I walk out on the floor and to the table. "Hey guys, how are you doing?" I ask. "I'll get you two cups of coffee," I said and walk to the front station. I walk back to the table and put the coffees down in front of each one.

"Hey, Sage, how goes it this morning?" asks Jack with his New Jersey accent.

Jack is the all-American dream with his blonde hair, blue eyes, and Armani wire-framed eye glasses. He wears perfectly pressed white shirts, fashionably oversized. And always an abstract tie decorated with wavy lines and amoeba-like curves.

"Sage, how are you?" asks Don. Don is a musician at heart, but works as a stockbroker because it comes easily to him. He has a wife and new baby. Don shows me pictures of her. She has a smile just like his, from ear to ear.

"Guys, are we healthy today or unhealthy?" I ask. I stand at the table looking at the front door. There is a man waiting to be seated. "Wait a minute. I'll be right back." I walk half way to the front door and pick up menus from the clear plexiglass menu holder. "How many?" I scream at the front door.

"Two of us, I'm waiting for someone," he says. "I'll put you right here and you can watch the front door. Do you want coffee?" I ask.

"Yes, coffee please," he says. "I'll be right back," I say. I walk down the aisle to the guys. "What do you guys want this morning?"

"I'm going to have Raisin Bran, rye toast with that whipped butter stuff, and preserves, the special one in the plastic pot. How's the fruit looking this morning, Sage?" Jack asks.

"If you order fruit, I'm going to go in the back and get it. You know that stuff up in the case looks anemic. I'm scared of it," I say and laugh.

"You probably should be. Miss Iggy probably puts that preserv-a-fruit stuff on it to keep the color so she can keep selling it, eh Sage?" Jack asks.

"How do you guys know all of our secrets? What do you feel like this morning, Don?" I ask.

"I wish we could have something like a natural disaster; what a lousy morning. Anyway I'm gonna have a happy stack, with the usual," Don answers.

"Do you want bacon or sausage," I ask. "Last time I got sausage, it hit Jack on the cuff," he laughs. "He gets that again, Sage, and I want a lobster bib," Jack says adjusting his cuffs.

"Yes sir," I say. "You want whites with that, Don?" "Of course, I want the whites. I have to watch my girlish figure," says Don.

"Yeah, he's got to watch it expand," says Jack. Jack has a great personality. I waited on him for more than two years, before he brought his boyfriend in here. The guy is better looking than I am. They have a beautiful house at the beach. I saw the pictures and it was all very impressive. Matty doesn't have a clue.

One day he was with a woman in her mid-thirties, like him. Matty circled the table a few times. She asked me and I told her it was his ex-wife and they were discussing an increase in the alimony payments. Don, Jack, and I all laughed the next day.

"I'll be back," I say. I walk away from the table and into the kitchen to hang the check. "What's thiz?" Rey asks. "You know who it is, thin cakes. He wants thin pancakes," I explain.

"Que, why you do this?" he asks. "Please, Rey. Pancakes

thin, tortilla-like. You know the way he likes them. All you have to do is flatten them on the grill. You know how he likes them," I say.

"Sage, you always make differently," he says. "Go ahead and say it, Rey. You know you want to. After today you have two days off from me, which should make you happy. Go ahead and call me la diablita, you know it'll set you free," I say.

"Ay," he says. He turns to the grill and pours out the cakes. I watch him as he flattens the bubbles. He knows I'm watching him. I have a bad habit of standing in the window and waiting for my food.

"We have other customers out here, Sage," Matty says. She practically spits out my name from those coral lips.

I walk to the coffee machine and pick up a coffee cup stored underneath in the hard green plastic crate, used in the dishwasher. Twirling the cup around in my hand, I check for lipstick stains. A lot of the time lipstick makes it through the dishwasher. They're supposed to bleach them out and disinfect them, but they don't. I walk to the table where the man is waiting for his friend.

"Here you go," I say. I place the coffee to his right. "You haven't seen a blonde guy, tall, and medium build?" he asks.

"No, but we're not easy to find. When you come here, you have to know where you're going," I say. "Did you tell your friend we're not on the main street? We're on Second Street, a side street, one block south?"

"Have you got a phone?" he asks. "Down the aisle, through the door, and on your left," I say. "Keep an eye out for me, will ya?" he asks. He walks briskly to the aisle and disappears, his necktie fly- ing over his shoulder as he rounds the corner and turns left.

"Of course," I say. I walk into the back kitchen through the swinging door and to the back refrigerator. I pull it open with the chrome handle, and look on the third shelf. Lulu has labeled where everything belongs in the back refrigerators. Of course, she took for granted that everyone who works here is able to read English. Most of the guys can speak it to a degree, but to read it is a joke. The fresh fruit is on the strawberry and avocado shelf. Close enough, I suppose. I fill the fruit cup way above the brim, and try to make an assortment with the oversized stainless steel spoon. I slam the door shut, and Freddy is behind it.

"Hey, you scared me, don't do that," I snap. "Special customers," he says grinning. "Regulars," I say. "I'll bet they're men," he says licking his lips. "Move it, Freddy. I have to get back on the floor. Matty is riding her broom today, one of the guys is married, and the other one is gay," I say.

"The hell with you," he screams in my face and walks away. He walks to the burners and puts a big wooden oar in the soup stirring it. Freddy is high yellow, almost a mulatto. If he were darker, I would think he was chanting voodoo incantations over the chicken soup.

"Loco," I say to myself. Everyone here calls him crazy and that's because he isn't all there. I walk out of the back, and the food is ready.

"Pick up, Sage," I hear through the wall of the kitchen. And then I hear the ding as the knife blade hit the heat lamp. "Pick up," Rey says smiling.

"Pick up, pick up, Sage, pick up," I say imitating his thick accent.

"Thin and hot, number one," Rey says. "Thanks, Rey," I say. I pick up the plates. Pulling the pan- cake syrup out of the matzo balls where we put it to warm it up, I splash some hot water on my hand. And I don't feel it. I have waitress hands,

83

immune to the heat. I walk out of the kitchen with Jack and Don's food in my hands.

"Watch for me," Matty barks at me as she walks by me quickly. I put the food down on the table. "Whatever I ate is going right through me," she says. I watch her red head walk through the kitchen and hang a right to the bathroom.

"Happy stack and whites to you," I say placing it in front of Don. "Raisin Bran, nonfat milk, rye toast with less fatty whipped butter and strawberry preserves. And I got this fruit out of the back, it's beautiful," I say.

"Thanks, Sage," says Don. "You're one in a million," says Jack. I walk back into the kitchen. "What did you do to her food, Rey?" I ask. "Mucho grease in the potatoes, always there," he says. He motions with his finger to behind me.

"Babe, can I get some coffee for my partner, he finally showed up," the customer says.

"Sure," I say. I follow him to the table. "Good morning, would you like coffee?"

"Please, it's my first cup of coffee for the day, I need it," he says. I walk back to the coffee station and pick up a coffee cup. I twirl the rim in my view. I'm safe, no lipstick stains. I pour the coffee a half-inch from the rim. As I walk out of the kitchen, I see Chester walk in the front door. I point to Matty's station. He doesn't sit in my station. I place the coffee in front of the guy and walk up to the front of the restaurant. In the booth next to this junior station which is built high on the wall in cherry wood stained plywood, Chester sits facing the door.

"Coffee?" I ask in a flat tone. "Yeah," Chester says as he nods his head. "Matty here?" He asks.

"She's in the bathroom," I reply. "Are you going to wait for them?" I ask. I try not to look into his sour, old face.

Chester is one of Matty's regulars. I refuse to wait on him.

I will pour him a cup of coffee to be decent, but no more. He sits in the booth with an unread newspaper next to him. He waits for the three hens. Age spots decorate his wrinkled face. He has a nose that has expanded to greatness in his eighty something years. His heavy eyelids hang low over his generic brown eyes. He continually clears his throat, in a rhythmic and annoying manner.

On a day when Matty called in sick, I poured him a cup of coffee. And then I took his order for an English muffin with butter on the side and no jam. They keep the toaster behind the dish out window on the cold side. The cold side is logically the side which sandwiches, salads, and bread come out of. The hot side is where the grill is, and the line where they store the day's specials and all other hot food. I waited for ten minutes for Chester's English muffin. I stood looking at the toaster, and then I went out and poured coffee for everyone. When I left the kitchen, Chester went into it. Eddy handed him the English muffin and he walked to his booth with it. He wouldn't accept any more coffee from me. When I walked into the kitchen, Eddy smiled over the dish out window. He thought it was funny. Chester complained about me up at the deli when he left, I had no defense. I won't wait on Chester anymore. His dollar tip doesn't mean that much to me.

The front door opens up, and the three hens walk in the door. As they join Chester in his booth, I look to the back of the restaurant for Matty. These women are everything I know that my mother is not. They do not wear lotus pink lips, but feathered coral which embodies the loss of the sweet bird of youth.

Matty will be gone for a while. It takes her at least ten minutes to pull off her two girdles and one pair of support panty hose. In the private stall of the women's bathroom, she has a fight on her hands. She physically fights with the danish, muffins, and grilled knockwurst sandwiches on kaiser rolls which are attached to her hips.

I walk to the booth and interrupt their irritating chatter. "Where's Matty?" asks April. She looks at me through her large round clear framed glasses, and dyed grey and white helmet hair style. "Is she sick again?"

"No, she's in the back. Do you want hot water?" I ask April. I knew she did by the way she already had her used cloudy zip lock plastic bag on the table with her bag of Irish break- fast tea and a handful of vitamins she takes for a longer life. She needs to live longer in order to find a new husband. The old one was running one night on a residential street where the houses are built high up on the flood plain. No one could see his body until the next morning. Rigor mortis had set in. I heard he looked like one of those statues at the wax museum. It was a closed casket.

"I want real coffee this morning, honey," says May, with her light brown hair styled like an Eva Gabor wig.

May is all right. She comes in here on the weekend with her husband. I can't imagine working hard your entire life and then having to share a breakfast. They are cheap, a buck from the two of them.

"I want hot tea this morning, with sweet and low," says June. June wears oversized T-shirts and leggings and has finger length dark brown hair. She's the youngest in the group and has a job. Her rich husband set her up in a nail salon, to keep her out of the mall. She looks at my hands as I put the hot pot in front of her.

"Matty will be right here," I say. I walk away to the two guys who finally linked up, and look at their coffee levels while I walk by the table.

"Can we get more coffee, honey?" the first one asks. "Sure," I say. I have a pot of regular, and a pot of decaf in my hands. I pour their coffee, and then walk back to the stockbrokers hidden behind the high walls.

"More coffee?" I asked at the table. "None for me, thanks, Sage," Jack says. "It was a wonderfully dietetic breakfast. Can we leave the check here?" he asks.

"No more coffee for me," Don says. He reaches across the booth for his jacket.

"Thanks, Sage," Don says. "Wait guys," I say. "Do you guys want it this morning?" "Yeah, everything helps," says Don. "Here we go," I say. I touch each of their shoulders with my hand and close my eyes for a second. "There we go, positive karma," I say.

"Thanks, Sage," says Don. "But keep some of it for yourself, don't give it all away," says Jack. He walks out of the restaurant behind Don.

"Bye guys," I scream after them. "We love ya," screams Jack. He pushes the door open and walks out following behind Don.

Those words, those serious words are thrown around today like a dirty Frisbee at the beach in the summer.

Eleven

I NEVER PURPOSELY SET out to hear the three ugliest words come out of Tomas' mouth. It just happened. Four months, fifteen days, and some odd number of both hours and minutes, he sprang those words. Those three words affected me like a paper cut which won't stop bleeding through the straight and clean wound.

In this life, my grandmother never found her peace. She was a vague figure who fed and clothed me, but rarely spoke. She belonged to the "actions speak louder than words" school, and so her use of words was limited. I would sit in her bedroom and look out the window to the rose garden. The tight bun on her head would swim around the garden, close to the leaves, thorns and buds she loved the most. In the hospital, she spoke more than I had ever heard her speak in person. There were so many words. I was scared. I always felt she had a gypsy mind and a closed heart.

Tomas and I had decided to spend Christmas together. He was sentimental, and I was practical. Since the death of my grandmother, I have spent every Christmas watching "It's A Wonderful Life" and eating three boxes of Fiddle Faddle. It was my comfortable tradition as I placed a fruit cake on the kitchen table for Grandma and Dad. She said he always loved it so. I can't remember, I don't remember. By morning I would watch the flies swarm above it, the maraschino cherries and assorted glazed fruit picked apart.

"What do you mean you don't do anything for Christmas?" he asked.

"It's just another holiday when the mail doesn't arrive and my checking account can't be pillaged," I snarled.

"Baby Bear, get in the mood," he pleaded. "It's gonna be our first Christmas together. You have to get in the mood," he said to me a week before the actual day.

"I'll try my best, Tomas. That's all I can say," I said. When I hung up the phone after our discussion, I felt a smile on my face. It would be a new experience.

My father died when I was still the age that an arts and crafts present would bring a smile to his face, as he looked up from the book in his hands. He never touched the present, only glanced at it. The amount of relationships I have had with men can be counted on one hand, and I have always managed to not be in one during any major holidays or sporting events.

"Can we cap the present at one hundred dollars?" I asked Tomas.

"No, Baby Bear," he said. He laughed. As we lay in bed that night, he held me close to his body. His warm, strong body filled with body tics which would emerge, and come alive. There were some mornings I would wake up bruised, from his elbow or knee. I got out of bed that night and put his arm delicately back on the sheets. I tip-toed across the bedroom and picked up his shirt. An extra-large T-shirt and a size thirty-six waist, those were his measurements. I climbed back into bed and fell asleep memorizing his sizes.

The next day, I made the trip to the mall. I learned that I know just about as much when it comes to shopping for men, as I know about the mechanics of a car engine. Large shops filled with dark patterns in black and brown and manly colors hung on the walls from chrome hangers.

"Can I help you?" the salesman asked. "Yes," I said. "He wears an extra-large T-shirt, and a size thirty-six waist. Those were the numbers I got off of his clothing last night."

"Well, he's a big one. What do you like to see him wear?" the salesman asked.

"He's a bouncer, so probably work clothes. Yeah, that'll be good, if I get him work clothes."

"Two pairs of jeans, how about the color?" he asked. "We have black, blue, and white. Which color?"

"How about one black and one blue," I said. "And a few over- sized white shirts," I said thinking about the way the shirts fall off of Jack, my morning regular.

One hundred and sixty-seven dollars later I walked out of the store. I drove home thinking about the look on his face.

On Christmas day, I woke up to loud knocking at the back of the house. I got out of bed, and walked through the house to the back door.

"I've been knocking on the door for about twenty minutes. Didn't you hear me?" he asked. He walked by me pushing me out of the way with his arms full of grocery bags.

"What time is it?" I asked. "It's afternoon, on our first Christmas." He bent over and kissed me on the top of my head. "I called, but there was no answer. I thought you might have gone out, or you were lost in your fathers' books again."

"No, I've got to go out. Do you need any help?" I asked ignoring his jealous comment on my books and reading.

"Where do you have to go? I thought all of your relatives were dead. Is it someone from work?" he asked anxiously.

"It's my other tradition at Christmas. I go to the cemetery and visit all of them. It's a habit, but I have to get some flowers from the garden. Do you need anything?" I asked. I walked by him on my way to the back yard.

"Where are you going?" he asked. "You need to go back there? But I've got a surprise for you back there. It's one of your presents." "I won't look. Let me just go out there, for a minute," I said. I didn't want to ruin my surprise. I was now looking forward to this day.

"Stay here," he said. Tomas walked out the back door, and down the

90

stairs.

I heard him speak through the kitchen window that doesn't close completely. It's swollen from the last rain, always swollen in Lala Land.

"Here we go," Tomas said. He walked through the door. "Look Steinbeck. It's your Mommy."

"How cute, Tomas," I said. I bent over to touch the black and white puppy. "He is so soft, like a baby chick."

"This is surprise, number one," he said. "When you're gone, I'll get everything ready. It's gonna be a great night. Hurry back." He kissed me on the forehead.

"A few hours, that's all it'll take," I said. I showered quickly, watching the puppy stare at me through the clean shower door. "He's following me," I yelled from the bedroom.

"That's great," Tomas yelled from the kitchen. The puppy followed me into the kitchen. "Have you seen the newspaper?" I asked. "You don't have time to sit down and read it, we're on a schedule," he said.

"Tomas, I want to wrap the flowers in it. Grandma used to do it, and it's just a habit I can't break," I said.

"By the back door, I saw some. I only got a turkey breast, I figured we didn't need the whole turkey," he said. He unpacked the grocery bags.

"That's fine," I said. "And the shears, back porch also, now that I think of it. I'll leave through the back yard. It won't take me long. I should be back before night falls."

Walking in the back yard, I felt Grandma. I stood next to her rose bushes and smelled the same warm, sweet, rose perfume that she had on her every time she came up from the garden. I held the bud in my left hand and cut at an angle with my right hand. The thorns made a jagged cut on the outside of my forearm. Holding the cut roses in the opened-up newspaper, I walked back up to the kitchen.

"What did you do, Sage?" Tomas asked. "Oh, don't use this sink, go into the bathroom."

I wiped the blood off on the newspaper. The blood coagulated at the seam of the cut. "I'll be back, Tomas," I said. I walked out of the door with my purse and keys in one hand, and the newspaper-filled with roses in the other.

Driving through the lazy day of Christmas on the freeway, I thought of my perfect evening. The sun shined lightly in the winter sky, and I followed it on my way to the cemetery. I saw the flesh-colored iron gates, and the topiary styled Bonsai bushes in front of the gates. Driving on the gentle black concrete, I found the "Immaculate Conception" section where my grandmother, father, and Rose of Sharon are buried. I parked the car and carried the roses covered in newspaper. The headstones were plain, with no adjectives, only the facts.

"Today I'm going to read from Travels with Charley. Daddy, I can't ever remember seeing you read this one, but I found it on the top of the armoire. I'll never know why you left it there, and why Grandma let it remain there. Here we go, now listen." Under the tall tree I sat with the leaves blowing down on me, reading to my grandmother, father, and Rose of Sharon. "When the virus of restlessness begins to take possession of a wayward man, and the road away from Here seems broad and straight and sweet, the victim must first find in himself a good and sufficient reason for going. This to the practical bum is not difficult. He has a built-in garden of reasons to choose from. Next he must plan his trip in time and space, choose a direction and destination. And last he must implement the journey. How to go, what to take, how long to stay. This part of the process is invariable and immortal. I set in down only so that newcomers to bumdom, like teen-agers in new-hatched sin, will not think they invented it.'"

An airplane flew low over the cemetery in line with the land- ing paths on LAX, and I felt a gust of wind under the old tree as I read the wise words.

"Hi Grandma and Daddy. I wish you both a Merry Christmas, I miss you both, and I love you both even though I never knew you," I said. "Rose of Sharon I miss you so much it hurts me every time I think of

you."

I placed the roses on the headstones. They made shapeless shadows under the winter sun. I placed my hand on Rose of Sharon's gravestone. I felt the cold stone and imagined her warm thoughts and wishes. After a quick Hail Mary and a stumbling Our Father, I walked away from the gravestones which are isolated by empty places on one side. I drove home by the side streets watching the oil derricks along Stocker, and the people walking to their trash cans with discarded wrapping paper stuffed and falling out of the royal blue trashcan. It was after dusk and the silhouettes fell against the indigo blue of the sky. I walked up the walkway and heard yelling escape from the keyhole. I made out the words of the anger as I turned the knob, and opened the door. "Stupid dog, stupid dog," Tomas yelled down at the puppy cowering at his feet. "Bad dog, bad dog." Tomas looked at me as I walked in the door.

"What's wrong, Tomas?" I asked. "The dog pissed in the house," he said.

"He's only a puppy," I said. "He has to learn, Sage. Train them while they're young, or else they'll never pay attention to you. You have to be firm, Sage. You don't understand," he said.

"Tomas, he's only a little dog. He'll learn, if you give him a chance. If you scold him or hit him, he'll be hand shy his entire life. We want him to be a people dog, not some unhappy dog who bays at the moon and sleeps outside," I said. I looked over to the table, set for our first holiday dinner. "Tomas, it looks beautiful." "I've been ready for over an hour. What took you so long?" he asked.

"I drove home on the side streets," I said. "You said you'd be home before the sun went down. You managed to ruin that surprise. I was worried about you," he said.

"Sorry," I said. "That's all right," he said. He walked up to me and hugged me, squeezing me tightly. "We didn't need margaritas on the back stairs for sunset on our first Christmas, anyway." He bent his head close to mine and kissed me on the top of my head. "Sorry," I said. I felt a

wrinkle surface on my forehead. "Wash your hands and clean up. I'll finish setting the table and put the dog out so he doesn't learn to beg from the table," he said. "Go clean up," he said. He pointed in the direction of the bathroom.

"Yes, sir," I said half-joking. I washed my hands and my face, and walked back out into the kitchen. "Well, where is it?" Tomas asked. "Where's what?" I asked. "You didn't go into the bedroom, did you?" he asked.

"No, I just washed my hands and face. I'm starving, can we eat?" I asked.

"Your surprise is on the bed, go in and look at it. I'm sure you'll love it. By the time you come back out here, everything will be on the table," he said.

"If you insist," I said. I walked into the bedroom, and there was a silver box and bow on the bed. I opened the box, and there was a floral nightmare dress in the box. Long sleeved and looking like flowers that have made a journey through a wood chipper; it was not something I would have selected for myself. The dress had a black base and a high, Victorian neckline.

"What do you think?" he yelled from the other room. "It's lovely," I yelled. "Put it on," he said. "Yes, sir," I said. I peeled my comfortable clothes off and put on the well-meaning rayon dress. I walked into the kitchen. The puppy scratched at the back door. He was whining and crying.

"You look wonderful," he said. "Thanks, can we eat?" I asked. "Can I help you, Tomas?" "I don't need any help," he said. "Why don't you go have a seat?" he said. He pointed to the dining room.

I walked out to the dining room and slid onto the Gothic wooden chair. I looked at the table with the linen tablecloth from my grandmother's linen closet. The folds of the material have a slight yellow color. The smell of moth balls seeped up from the fringes hanging off of the ends of the table. The table was set with the formal china and cut glass which had lived on

94

the top shelves of the kitchen cabinet, since my grandmother died. The crystal goblets glared against the overhead light which beamed down on them. All of the food was covered with aluminum foil, shiny side up.

"How does it look?" Tomas asked. He walked in with a large platter. "Can you move that thing over a little, no, not that, yeah, that's the one." He walked back into the kitchen.

"Are you sure you don't need any help?" I asked. I thought about those magical words of Steinbeck's' "the victim must first find in himself a good and sufficient reason for going," definitely an unnatural combination of words, practically stumbling over a front stoop. The words hung in my head and troubled me as I thought about my mother.

"What do you want to drink with your dinner?" he asked from the other room.

"What are you having, Tomas?" I asked. "I'm having wine," he said. "I'll have some wine, too," I said. "Are you sure you can handle it?" he asked. "Yes, I can," I said. "Here we go," he said walking out of the kitchen. He carried an opened bottle of wine in one hand, and two candle sticks in the other hand. "Now, this is a Christmas feast."

"It looks wonderful," I said. The puppy scratched at the back door.

"Let me put these down," he said. He put the candlesticks down on the table in the middle and the bottle of wine near him. "Now, the table looks perfect."

"It looks beautiful, Tomas. Thanks. I'm surprised," I said. "Why are you surprised? You don't think I'm capable of doing great things, just because I work as a bouncer?" he said attacking.

"I'm sorry. I didn't mean it to sound that way. I'm just surprised you did something this nice for me," I said. I attempted to save the night.

"I accept your apology. Wait a minute. It's too bright in here. Let me turn out the overhead light, but first," he said. He ripped all of the aluminum foil off of the dishes. He wadded it up in a big ball. I could hear Grandma cursing about not keeping the foil and rinsing it off so that it could be reused.

95

"It's wonderful," I said. "That's because I'm Mr. Wonderful," he said. "Wait a minute, look at me," he was adjusting the candles. "That's much better. I can see the light dance in your eyes and you look like such a lady in that dress."

"I feel very proper in this dress," I said. "Sage, you look absolutely beautiful. I like you so much, I just wanted to share it with you," he said.

We sat among the formalities of the dishes and glasses, listening to the whining of the puppy outside. I felt all grown up, like I was stuck in a picture somewhere and I was saying cheese and waiting for the flash bulb to go off in my eyes. Tomas ate his food, smiling at me as I ate the food he placed on my plate. We finished our meal and I swigged down the last amount of deep red wine in my glass.

"Why did you do that?" he asked. "I wanted to finish the glass to round out the meal," I said. "Do you know what sits at the bottom of everything you drink? Spit does. I never drink the bottom of anything, because it's mostly spit," he said with a serious look on his candlelit face. "I never finish a drink and that's the reason."

"Sorry, I never thought about it that much. I mean the spit be- longs to me, after all I was the only one drinking from the glass," I said.

"Let's open our presents," he said. He stood up from the table. "I put your presents on the table, over there."

"I left yours behind the couch," I said. I walked over to the couch. "What about the dishes?" I asked.

"You can do them later on," he said. He sat in the big black leather chair which looked so small when he dropped into it. "Yours are right there." He pointed to the table. "But the dress was also one of your presents," he said as he smiled.

"Here you go," I said as I handed him the five boxes. He opened the two big ones, the black and blue jeans. "Thanks, Baby Bear, I needed clothes." As I sat next to him on the big chair, he kissed my forehead.

Tomas doesn't like to kiss on the lips. There was some story about aunts and uncles who used to kiss him on the lips. He said it's disgusting.

He kisses me on the forehead or the top of my head, but never on the lips. Tomas also doesn't see the succulence in toes and sucking them or the sensual curve of the hand with it's hard and soft textures. There are days I miss the feel of soft fleshy lips next to mine. On some days, I kiss him on the lips while he is sleeping, just to feel their baby softness and forbidden nature.

"These three are mine? You are so generous," he kissed my cheek. "They're all the same, aren't they?" he asked.

"There are slight differences. Do you like them?" I asked. I sat by his side on the chair. "I like them. They're oversized."

"They're great," he said. He kissed me again on the forehead. "Open yours up," he said.

But you already got me the dress and the puppy, what more could you have gotten me, Tomas?" I asked.

"Just open the box, you'll see what I got you," he said. I opened the box, a set of knives in a block of wood. It even had a pizza cutter and a knife sharpener.

"Thanks, Tomas," I said. I kissed him on the cheek. We sat awkwardly in the big chair, our bodies touched. The puppy outside scratched at the door, and whined in the silence of this celebrated night.

"You haven't read my card, open it up. That's the biggest present," he said. He placed his arm around my shoulder.

I picked up and opened the white envelope with the solitary initial S handwritten on the outside of the it.

"That's the real present, not the puppy, dress, or knives," he said.

I opened the Christmas card with the man and woman hold- ing hands on the face of it. As I opened the card, I read the printed sappy greeting. And then under it, was the present. The three words, "I love you," were hand written.

"Tomas," I said. I was lost for words. "I wanted you to know how I feel," he said. "But we haven't known one another that long," I said. "I know you're the one for me, and I know I'm the one for you," he said.

"Tomas, I'm serious," I said. "I don't know what to do." "I said I would save you and that's exactly what I'm going to do. I want to protect you and keep you safe. I'll always be around for you," he said. He pulled my head to his chest where I listened to his heart beat.

"But, Tomas," I said. "What's the first thing that comes to your head when you read those three words?" he asked.

"Light years," I said. I grasped for words. "That's not what I wanted to hear," he said. He moved my head away from his body. "I'm here to save you, because you have those eyes that scream out save me. Baby Bear, I'll always be here."

That night in bed, I fell asleep in the warmth of his wing-like arm. I dreamed I was stuck in the cosmos, hearing the words "I love you" in blinding repetition. The puppy slept on the bed at my feet, just this once.

Twelve

I WATCH A WOMAN close to my age suffering with the mechanics of a baby carriage as she attempts to walk through the front door. I look at her glassy brown eyes through her wire-framed glasses. She walks in rolling it, and looks around the restaurant.

"One and a half," I say. I approach her. "Yes, please," she says in a small voice. "Here you go," I say. I place one menu on the table. "Do you need a highchair?"

"Yes, please," she says. "Abby, you'll sit in the high chair, baby, won't you?" she says to the child, looking for complete dialogue.

I walk over to the station and pull up the highchair which is tangled in a piled-up mess. I struggle with the pretty blonde wooden prop. And I think of the cup at home and question whether or not it has changed color. On a day when the demons play tag in my head, I bring the high chair back to the table.

"Thanks, can I get some decaf?" she asks. She lifts the baby out of the carriage and puts it in the high chair. "I'll need a couple of minutes," she says to me as I stare at her in her struggles. She puts a terry cloth bib with pink plastic piping around the edges on the baby.

"Here you go," I say. I walk back to the kitchen and stand just behind the wall. I watch this pretty woman without any makeup and with hair cut very short in an unflattering yet instant style. She talks with her baby and places Cheerios on the naked table.

I think about my mother and those lips of hers. The one thing I do remember is that she always was well groomed when she left the house with complete make-up and hair, all the way down to her manicured nails. As a child, I don't believe I ever saw her fingernails nude or dirty.

"Can't you see the customers standing at the front door?" Matty blazes at me. "Do you want to wake up and try doing your job?" she says. "Hello, two?" she asks.

I stick my head out to look at the customers. It's Paul and his Nordic-blonde daughter, Kelly. I smile and wave at them, he points at me. Matty walks them to a booth in my section, and when she turns around, she looks like a gargoyle hanging off of a gothic-style building, ugly and menacing. For a split second, her eyes scare me. But I've had it and I'm an inch away from telling her to fuck off. I don't have a life sentence; I'll be up for parole soon; or else I'm going to make a break for it. I'm not a lifer, I repeat these words to myself daily.

"Hey guys, how are we doing this morning?" I ask. I stand at the table. "Do you want coffee?" I ask Paul.

"We're not doing that well," he says. Kelly sits next to her father. He brushes the hair away from her forehead. "We didn't want to get out of bed. Kelly, did you show Sage what outfit you picked out for yourself today? She was absolutely convinced that turquoise and cherry red would match. So this is what we've worn to breakfast this morning. Kelly, why don't you show Sage what you did to your Barbie doll?" he asks. He looks down at her.

"Hey, Kelly, what did you do?" I say bending down low to the table to see her at eye level.

"See," she says. I look at the doll. Barbie doesn't have a nose. There is a little hole where the nose should have been on her plastic face.

"She looks very nice," I say. "Think so. I think so," she says. She turns her head and buries her face in her father's shirt.

"We were playing with the scissors. Her mom didn't have time for her this weekend, so she's a little upset. I think she heard me talking to her mom on the phone. But I don't know how she figured out what rhinoplasty is? How are you doing, Sage?" he asks.

"Wonderful, things are," I say. "La, la, la, la, food, I want food," Kelly says. "Kelly, we're going to feed you. How about some pancakes. Baby, do you want some pancakes this morning?" he asks her. "Give her a short stack."

"No," she says. "How about two pancakes? That's what you want, right Kelly?" he asks.

"Pancakes," she says still buried in her father's shirt. "She's been sensitive to the word short ever since we came back from the doctor for her physical," he says. "And I'll have bacon crispy, scrambled hard and rye toast with butter on the side."

"Yes, sir," I say. I walk to the station and pour his cup of coffee. Paul is bent over having a conversation with Kelly. I don't interrupt them when I put the coffee down. They are sweet together. Even after a divorce, he is present in her life. He asked me out once, but I told him about Tomas. You've got to like someone who names their daughter after all of the sluts in his old high school. He just wanted to make sure there would be a place for her in society.

As I walk into the kitchen, I hear a loud chomping. Matty is snacking on whole wheat toast, buttered and cut up in little squares. I look at her and I can see the plate of her dentures moving as her jaw sits still.

"My back is starting to go out. I had to have something to eat with my medicine," she says justifying her snack.

"Whatever," I say. My approach is to dismiss her justification. I have never worked some place where all of these women have to justify their food intake, like I'm the diet police. I walk over and hang the tag in front of Rey. He places the freshly fried bacon on the dish out window.

"Want some?" asks Rey.

"No, thanks," I say. I smell the salt and grease rise up to the heat lamps. "That's not what I need today."

"That woman with the baby is getting up and going to the station," Matty says standing in front of her plate of toast.

I walk over to the woman's table. "Can I help you?" I ask. "I just needed sweet and low," she says. "But I'm ready to order."

"What would you like this morning?" I ask. "What kind of fresh fruit do you have?" she asks. The woman feeds the baby Cheerios by hand, putting the saliva-covered ones from the table back in the baby's mouth.

"We have a fruit cup. Its part canned and part fresh," I say. "Can you pick out the canned fruit?" she asks. "No, I can't. We do have cantaloupes and grapefruit," I say. I hear Rey ring the bell in the kitchen. My food is ready.

"I'll have a half a cantaloupe and a bagel. Do you have any crackers I can feed the baby?" she asks.

"We have water, onion, and egg bagels. And do you want it toasted?" I ask. "Cream cheese is a dollar extra." I ignore the cracker question. I have to get into the kitchen before he starts to ring the heat lamp again.

"Water bagel toasted, no cream cheese," she says. She leaves

102

the menu on the table and begins to play and talk to the baby. I pick up the oversized plastic laminated blue menu off of the table. Cheerios fall to the ground. The woman doesn't notice. I watch her play with the baby. There is a feeling of alienation when I see her sweetly touch the baby.

As I walk into the kitchen, I hear the blade against the heat light. Matty stands in front of the coffee machine, a hollow chewing sound coming out of her mouth. Her fingers are covered with butter fat.

Miss Lee walks into the kitchen. Matty shoves her toast under the coffee machine.

"Good morning, Miss Lee," Matty says. Toast crumbs decorate the corners of her mouth.

"Morning," Miss Lee says. She stands and waits as Matty pours her coffee. "We need more plates? And soup spoons?" she asks accusingly.

"We keep running out of soup spoons during lunch. I think the boys are throwing them out. We have to go in the back and fish them out of bus trays during our busiest time of the day. We don't want to lose any more business. Miss Lee, you know we want everyone to be happy . . .", said Matty scram- bling for words.

I pick up my food, and leave the kitchen listening to Matty kiss up to Miss Lee for her job. Kelly is playing with her doll, walking it across the table. Paul talks to Kelly as I approach the table with the food.

"Kelly, put your doll away," he says. She leans the doll against the wall. I glance at Barbie. She has lotus-pink lips. I never noticed that before. I put the plates on the table. Paul starts to butter her pancakes and then he cuts them up in small squares.

"Tell me when, with the syrup, Kelly," he says. He holds the syrup over the pancakes.

"When," she says after one drop. "Ha, ha, ha." "No more, baby?" he asks easily. "More, please, Daddy," she says laughing.

I walk away from the table, feeling as if I have invaded the intimacy of a father and daughter through a window of their big house. When I think of my father, I think of his books and his magnificent hands turning the pages. He was always caught up in the creations of other people.

"Sage, long time waiting," I hear from the kitchen. I walk into the kitchen. Matty is up at the hen's table clucking with them. Rey stands in front of the toaster.

"Thiz is cold," he says pointing at the bagel. "Don't worry about it," I say. I pick it up and put it down on the counter with two jellies and butter on the side. I open the ice box below, and take out a cantaloupe. As I cut it, the juice escapes with the seeds. I scoop the seeds out and throw them out in the tray used as a trash can. I walk out of the kitchen and to the woman's table.

"Here we go," I say. I place the bagel and melon on the table. I watch the woman look so lovingly into the eyes of the baby. "Here are the crackers," I say. I take them out from my apron pocket. I walk to the front station to get the coffee pots and pour coffee for Paul and the woman. I walk back to the station; the hens are talking about the race track and the lotto. They're dreaming about their winnings. Some people need less; I think to myself. I stand at the station, staring at the clock on the opposite end of the restaurant. One hour has passed since the restaurant opened.

"Hey, Sage," a young voice says to me. "Hi, Donna and Dina," I say. "Where's your station, honey?" asks Donna, the mother. "We want to sit with you," says Dina, the daughter.

"I'm back here, against the wall. Anywhere you want, I'll find you. That's two decafs, right?" I ask.

I walk to the table and place the cups of coffee down. "How are you doing, honey?" Donna asks. Donna is a large sized woman with beautiful black hair held back in a hair band and an impeccably detailed made up face. She puts her warm hand over mine and holds it for a second.

"You look great, Sage. We were here one day last week, but we didn't see you. I guess it was your day off," Dina says. "Mom didn't like the waitress very much. She never brought us any pickles."

"Are we going to do the usual?" I ask. "That's why we like you. And the fact that you're so sweet," Donna says.

"I'll be back," I say. Donna and Dina attended my grandmother's funeral. They were the only people there other than myself and the mortician, whose first job it was. Each one stood by my side, as they wheeled the casket out of the church because there were no pallbearers. I look at them and I wish I belonged with them. Donna is a housewife and Dina is a makeup artist in the studios. She brings me extra makeup sometimes. I accept it thankfully. "Rey, I need a number one, dry. And a white meat turkey, dry, with aus jus on the side on a toasted plain bagel."

"Where's the check? You know I need to see the check," he says. "What is this, your day to make my life a living hell?" I raise my voice. "I'm writing the check now."

"Lulu said," he says standing at the slicer, slicing the meat for the sandwich. "Pick up. It's done."

"Where's the juice?" I ask.

"Not my job," he says smiling. "Next window." "Thanks," I say picking up the food from both sides of the dish out. I walk to the table with the pickles balancing on the side of the number one plate.

"You're great," Dina says. "She knows our order exactly. Who was that old shrew working anyway?"

"A lifer," I say. "Your makeup looks great. I like the darker shade on your lips; I didn't like that artificial light pink you were wearing," says Dina.

And I think about the lotus pink lipstick. High Frost, looking almost frosted, was the pink I wore. It was a sweet pink lipstick, named lotus. It was fate when I saw the name. I had to wear it. I had to wear it even though I didn't feel like myself when I wore it. I felt like I was someone else.

When I was twelve years old, I walked down the street from our house to Sunset Boulevard and took the 91 bus I had traveled on with my father into Hollywood. I looked around the bus at the faces of people and out the window at the people down below. People stared straight ahead on the bus, not looking around. I exited the bus at Vine Street, and crossed the street at the light. I walked into the Broadway Hollywood, with the fine jewelry on my right side.

Between the glass and brass of the cosmetic counters, I found what I was looking for. Beautiful women stood behind the counters, smiling through lined lips and long black eyelashes. I stood awkwardly with my navy-blue corduroys, light blue and white striped T-shirt up to my neck. Tan colored Earth shoes made my feet appear extra-large. I smelled the sweet jasmine perfumes and rose oils as I walked along the cases.

"Can I help you?" asked a woman who looked like an angel. She had platinum blonde hair cut softly around her face. Flawless skin, heart-shaped lips and hazel eyes with green flecks in them, made up her face.

"Makeup," I said timidly. "Darling, do you want to be made up?" she asked. "Yes, ma'am," I said. "Well have a seat, darling," she said. She pointed to the stool in front of the case. "I'll make you right up."

I sat in the seat and she flew around me. She pulled my hair back in a tortoise shell hair clip and stood in front of me. As she looked at me, she appeared to be having a private conversation with herself. I sat in the chair and tried not to move, watching her concentration. When I looked in the mirror, I looked almost beautiful. My lips were light pink, and my skin was flawless with face powder. My eyes had an almond shape to them, outlined in chocolate brown.

"Darling, you look like an angel," she cooed. "Thanks," I said. "How much is the lipstick?" I asked. "Eight dollars," she said. "I have ten dollars," I said. "I would like the lipstick." "Sure, darling," she said. She wrapped the lipstick back in the box and put it in a bag. "Come back in a few years, darling. You're going to be a head turner."

I walked out of the store pushing the brass handrails on the glass of the door. The bus was on the corner and I ran against the "Don't Walk" light to catch it. I watched in the mirror from my seat behind the bus driver my adult look.

When I got off of the bus at my stop, I walked slowly up the two blocks to the house. Grandma was out in the garden. I walked down the stairs to show her my new look. She was among the sanctity her roses.

"What have you done?" she asked. "Nothing," I said. "Look at you. You look like a tramp. Take that slop off of your face," she screamed.

"I look pretty," I screamed in the dampness of the garden. "You look like a whore," she screamed. Grandma took her gloved hand and smeared the lipstick. Thorns and stems were stuck to the glove. "Look at those pink lips, only a whore wears pink like that."

I ran upstairs. In the bathroom mirror, I saw the thin line of blood from a thorn on her glove. I placed the lipstick and the hair clip in an old cigar box, filled with funeral cards of my father and sister, and the newspaper clipping of John Steinbeck's death.

"Definitely the darker shade on you, Sage," Donna says.

"Sage, the darker color looks more dramatic on you," Dina agrees. "Besides, blackened colors are in right now."

I walk away from the table. I look around the restaurant, and the woman with the baby is struggling on her way out the door. "We'll see you next time, Sage," says Paul. He walks up to me with Kelly, holding her hand. "What do you say, Kelly?" "Thank you," she says from behind her father's legs. "I'll see you guys, later," I say waving to them. They walk out of the door. I turn around and look at the clock. I feel the demons around me, laughing and smiling as they play tag.

Dina and Donna laugh at their table. They are a mother and daughter out for an early morning breakfast. I envy them. A middle-aged woman walks in the door. I walk up to her. She wears the wrong shade of pink.

Thirteen

"HELLO. ONE?" I ASK. The woman is about my height, with similar cheekbones and a large smile. She smiles at me when I approach her.

"I'm waiting for someone. Can I sit somewhere where I can see the door?" she asks.

"Sure," I say. I walk her to a booth in my station, with a view of the door. She sits in the booth. "Would you like some coffee?" I ask.

"Please." She unfolds a newspaper on the table. "Can I get some Sweet and Low?" she asks.

"Yes, of course," I say handing her a few packets out of my pocket. I look at the newspaper in front of her. "What's that on the front page?" I ask.

"A story about an abandoned baby. They found this little girl in a trash can. She still had remnants of her umbilical cord attached to her. Poor little thing, to be left all alone in the world. Her mother must have been desperate. She must have been scared," the woman says and sips her coffee.

"The little girl's better off," I respond. "You don't have any children, do you?" the woman asks. "Do I look stupid? I wouldn't want to do that, ruin a child's life by bringing it into this world," I spit the words out in a surly tone. With my hand in my pocket, I feel for the postcard. It's still there.

"Parents have their reasons." "Excuses," I mumble under my breath. I walk away from the table and I look up at the clock. Matty stands at the table of the hens. I stand in front of the adding machine, looking out the front door.

The door swings open and Bertha walks in. She is another waitress who has worked here for a hundred years. She has a bag of kitty litter hung over her shoulder and held by her red nail polished inch and a half claws, the only stilettos she can still wear. She walks by me smelling of Avon perfume and Ban deodorant. Her bleached platinum blonde hair falls stiffly against her jaundiced complexion. Her two-pack-a -day cough with congestion and wheeze, makes me feel sick. I ignore her and her negativity caravan. She won't talk to me since I stopped buying Avon.

"Morning, Bert," says Matty. "Morning, Matty," says Bertha. "How are the kids?" "Little Rose and Daisy are great," says Matty.

"My big twenty-pound cat, Guido, had to go to emergency last night," says Bertha.

I listen to this trivial conversation. My mother cannot be this type of woman. She must be something different. I couldn't have a mother who is as content as these women, reading romance novels and being addicted to diet pills and Slim Fast shakes. I feel the postcard in my pocket and walk away.

"Excuse me, Miss. Could we get another coffee?" says the woman at the table. "My sister's here."

"Sure," I say. I pour the coffee and bring it to the table. "Do you need another menu?"

"No," says the second woman. "What are you gonna have, Sis?" "What are you having?" the first woman asks. "Can you

110

give us a moment, please?" the second woman asks. "Sure, no problem," I say. I walk away. The two sisters laugh their inherited giggles which they share from common blood. It echoes from the table.

I stand at my station and watch the clock. Today I woke up feeling as if the demons would be playing tag with me throughout the day and I was correct. I watch the two sisters share an intimacy of memories. Rose of Sharon and I would have been the greatest of friends. We would have had the same thing. We would have laughed and cried together. She would have been there when I was struggling to find my place in this world, because she too would have struggled with the same problems. As I listen to these women laugh and talk, I feel a piercing tingle in my ear, like swimmer's ear earned during a summer spent at the beach.

"Hey girlie girl, what's going on?" asks Cherry.

"Nothing," I answer. "You looked like your mind was a million years away. Sage, you had the most serious look on your face," she says.

"Nothing," I say. I see the squinty addictive look in her eyes she still has after nine months of sobriety. She places her hand on my shoulder and I look down at the pearlized white color on her nails.

"Is it the old bags?" she asks. Her pudgy cheeks and color-less lips ask in concern.

"You know how they are," I rejoin. "I get so tired." "You're not a lifer, Sage. You're not one of them. And they know that. Besides, they don't like anyone less than fifty," she says laughing. "There's something falling out of your pocket and you're gonna lose it."

"It's nothing," I grumble. "Just a postcard, nothing special." "Who's it from?" she asks. "My mother," I say. "Sage, I thought your mother was dead. I thought you had no living relatives," she says questioningly.

"I was wrong," I say. "I got a postcard from her." "Let me see it," she says. "It's not important," I argue. "Sage, just let me look at it," she says holding out her hand. "Where is she and where has she been?" she asks.

"It doesn't say any of that," I say. "I've got to take an order, Cherry. Let me go."

"Let me see it," she pleads. "Here," I say and hand it to her. I walk away to the table with the sisters.

"Have you decided?" I ask. "We're just gonna have the coffee, honey. Is that OK?" the first woman asks.

"No problem," I answer as I stand at the table feeling the warmth in their words. I place the check on the table and walk back to Cherry.

"Why is there a picture of Disneyland? I don't get it, Sage," she inquires. The postcard is in her hand. The creases from the crumbling have frayed the picture.

"I've never been there," I reply. "What are you talking about?" she asks. "Cherry, I've never been to Disneyland," I repeat. "You're a native Californian and you've never been there. That's so bizarre, Sage. I didn't even grow up here and I've been to Disneyland. What do you think she wants from you?" Cherry asks. "I don't know. I don't want to think about it. I've got too much stuff to think about today," I rebut.

"That's so weird, Sage. I wonder what she looks like? Where do you think she is?" Cherry asks.

"I don't really want to talk about this, Cherry. Not right now, I can't think about it." I hold my hand out for the postcard.

"Sorry, I'm just curious," she says apologizing. Cherry hands it back to me.

"It's funny, they have milk cartons for lost kids, but not for lost parents," I say and walk away from the station.

I look around at the restaurant. Matty and Bertha sit at a table and do their bitching and snitching. The hens and Chester walk out the door, waving at Matty. I stand at the station looking at the postcard from my mother.

Sage, I need to talk to you. Love, Mom XOXOXO

I wonder what type of evil woman she must be. She must be a nasty and cruel monster, incapable of giving love.

On the day after my mother disappeared, we were supposed to go to Disneyland. There were four tickets sitting on the kitchen table for Disneyland. Grandma was away. My father had no intention of going to Disneyland.

As afternoon approached and the western sun entered through the lace curtains, I sat on the orange-yellow wool couch reading a book. My father sat across from me reading The Pearl all day long. I felt hunger eat away at my insides and wondered if he would make me lunch.

"Daddy, are we gonna eat?" I asked. "As soon as I'm done with this book," he answered. I watched him read, leaning into the window light, one leg crossed over the other. His chest moved up and down, as his hands gripped the jacket of the book. I watched him lost in the words. He didn't say anything about Mom and nothing about Rose of Sharon. He closed the book and walked over to me.

"Sage, I want you to read this. I'll go make you supper and you study these words," he said.

Later that evening, I sat with my father at the table alone. The table was set for five people.

"Are there people coming?" I asked.

"Just the two of us," he said looking at the table. My father made stewed tomatoes and chipped beef over white toast.

"Why are there five settings?" I asked. "Because," he answered. He looked me in the eye with his warm dark eyes, and blinked slowly.

113

"Because we have set places for some of us, who can't be here today. Some people aren't strong enough to deal with real life."

"All right," I said. I didn't understand exactly what he was saying to me. "When will Grandma get home?" I asked.

"She'll be back soon," he said. "When are we gonna go to Disneyland?" I asked. "We aren't," he answered firmly. "But we have tickets, Daddy," I pleaded. "Just because you have something, doesn't mean you have to use it, Sage. I think it's better if we don't go," he said. "I'd rather sit here and read, wouldn't you?"

"But the tea cups, and the Dumbo ride. I heard all about it," I said. "If Mom was here, she'd take me. I know she would."

"We're not going," he replied firmly. "Mom will take me when she comes back," I screamed. "She's not here," he said. He turned to me and looked me in the eye. "I don't want to hear about your mother. She isn't here. She can't take you on the tea cups or any other ride. Our table will only be set for three now. Do you understand me, Sage?"

"No Disneyland. I get it," I answered. "Things will get better, if the clouds leave. I know you're too young to understand what I'm talking about. But Sage, things will get better. I stay in my books because of the security and wisdom of the words. It's a safe place to be. It's a good place to be." He touched my hand which rested atop the table. "You're too young to understand the clouds, but one day you'll be old enough. You'll grow up and you'll get your own set of clouds."

"Can I be excused?" I asked. "No, not yet. I want to talk to you. Did you memorize that little paragraph I showed to you earlier?" he asked.

"Not yet," I said. "Well go get the book, I want to read it to you," he said. I hesitated. "Go get the book, Sage," he repeated. I walked into the front room. There on the couch was the book, The Pearl. I carried it into the kitchen. At the doorway, I watched my father hold the plate from the place setting where my mother had always sat. He held the old china plate with the tiny rosebuds to his chest and sighed. He held that plate until he

114

realized I was watching him. Then he quickly put the plate on the table and as it hit the tablecloth it made a thump noise.

"Sage, hand me the book," he ordered. "I can read it," I replied. "I know you can, but I want to read it to you," he said. I silently handed the book to him. "I know you're too young right now, but one day it will all click into place. One day you will understand the clouds," he repeated. "This is the opening page from a beautiful book."

"I read it earlier," I said. "Listen to the words, Sage. I want you to listen to the words with your heart," he said ignoring me.

"Yes, sir," I said.

"'And, as with all retold tales that are in people's hearts, there are only good and bad things and black and white things and good and evil things and no in-between anywhere,'" he read. "I know you're too young, but it isn't true. Most of life is filled with grey. Clouds are grey and life is grey."

"I see," I said. "I think you're too young, too young to understand what has happened. One day you'll see it all," he replied.

"Can I be excused?" I asked. "Yes," he said. "But wait." He tore the page out of the book. "I want you to study this, study this your entire life. And when the clouds blow in, you'll think of this page."

He handed me the page from the book and I walked out the door.

"Goodnight, Daddy," I said. "I love you, Sage. I may not always say it, but I love you. I loved Rose of Sharon. I loved your mother in my own special way," he said.

"Goodnight, Daddy," I said. In the middle of the night, I got up for a glass of water. I walked to the doorway of the kitchen. A full moon hung low against the tall palm trees. It was shining through the open kitchen window. I saw my father holding the plate to his chest and silently sobbing at the kitchen table. I walked back to my bedroom, and held that page from the book in my hands as I prayed for the night to end.

The front door opens, and a man walks in the door. "Excuse me, have you got a bathroom?" he asks. "Through the back door and past the telephone," I say. I look around the restaurant. All of the booths are empty. Freddy the chef walks out of the kitchen and starts to write the specials on the board.

"Excuse me, Miss," Freddy says. "Yeah, what?" I ask. "How much are the stuffed peppers?" he asks. "Five and a quarter," I say. "And the chicken a la king?" he asks. "Same," I say. I stand next to him as he writes large loopy styled letters on the chalkboard.

"You smell good, what is that?" he asks. "My Sin," I reply. "I love you. You're not like the rest. You got a spirit, missy. Full of piss and vinegar, you're not like the rest of these old women," he says chuckling.

"Thanks. I feel so much better. I see life clearly now," I say sarcastically.

"Well anyway, the clouds are blowing out. It looks like we're gonna have a clear sky. And what a beautiful day it is," he says.

"What a beautiful day," I agree and walk away.

Fourteen

"IS PETER THE GREAT here yet?" asks Cherry.

"No," I say. "Sagey, are you having a bad day?" she asks. Cherry puts her arm around my shoulder, and steps in closer to me. "Things will work out; I know it doesn't seem that way now. Does that make you feel better?"

"No," I say. "I know. This day above all days you don't need mothering. Sorry, it's the co-dependent in me. I'm gonna get a cup of coffee and let you do your thing. If you need me, I'll be in the back, chain smoking," she says. "It's okay, kiddo."

I stand at the station and wait for customers. I have cabin fever and would bolt for the door except for the fact that my keys are locked up in my locker. If I was outside, I would stand and watch the clouds roll across the sky.

"Hi, Sage," says Kirsten. "Hello," says Monica. "Hi, guys," I say. "You're early. You want to sit in my station?" "Of course," says Kirsten, wearing her yellow-blonde hair up in a ponytail. "You're not looking happy today." She said this smiling at me with a curled lip.

"A lot of shit around this place. I should have been smart and gotten a job with my degree like you two. This job is for the birds," I answer.

"Oh yeah, we have great jobs. Didn't I tell you they cut me back to commission only? I'm cutting out and going horseback riding this afternoon," says Monica. Her red lipstick and naturally curly chestnut hair would ordinarily make her the type of woman I would hate. But Monica is sweet in a charming way.

"You probably make more money than we do, Sage," says Kirsten. Her hand taps the top of her black wallet.

"I've shook more hands and gone on more interviews in the last month than I did when I got out of Pepperdine," laments Monica.

"Let's change the subject," I say. "What do we want today?" I watch the front door open and a couple walks in the door.

Matty walks up to the front of the restaurant and greets the two people. She walks them to her station and seats them.

"It's not your fault. You just work with old women. There are plenty of waitress jobs out there. Anyone would hire you," replies Kirsten.

Monica and Kirsten are silent as Matty walks by the table.

"Didn't anyone tell her green eye shadow has been out for two decades? I would go crazy working here," laughs Monica.

"Yeah, she looks like the wicked witch of the west," Kirsten observes. "I want matzo ball soup and a diet coke."

"On my budget, I'm gonna have the same thing," Monica replies.

"Thanks, I'll be back," I answer. I walk into the kitchen and see Matty eating a cup of soup. She puts it in a coffee cup thinking no one will notice. "NO EATING ON THE FLOOR ON YOUR SHIFT." This is another rule Lulu has announced. I fill the two soup bowls. The matzo ball looks like a planet, with chicken broth sloshing around it and onto the plate. I carry the drinks on a tray in one hand and the two bowls balanced against one another in the other hand. I walk back to the table.

"Well, what was I to say?" asks Kirsten. "I haven't an answer," concludes Monica. "I was mute," Kirsten says. "Here we go." As I put down the soup bowls, they stop their conversation. "What did I interrupt?" I ask.

"Ask her," says Monica. "What do you think about pillow talk, Sage?" Kirsten asks. "Everyone does it," I answer. "I vote for the wordless grunters," says Monica. "You would," says Kirsten. "Monica likes them big and stupid." "I always get them that way. It's just the type of man I attract. I can't help it," Monica says laughing. She throws her head back and twirls a small section of her hair with her left hand. "I try for the brains, but they're not good-looking enough."

"Soft words," I say. "Baby talk," says Kirsten. "Big shoulders and big arms," Monica says. "Dumb-as-a-box-of-rocks, that's her preference," Kirsten says laughing.

"You two are awful," I say. I look around the restaurant; the place is empty except for my table and one other. I look at these two and I feel like we're sisters. They're always so happy and full of life. They've invited me out before, but I always declined. After Rose of Sharon died, I never wanted to have the feeling of a sister again. I had a friendship with a girl down the block from the house, Rosemary. She was like a sister, but we lost touch after college. I never made many close friends either. I didn't want someone else to replace the two of them. I always wanted to feel the pain, because at least I was feeling something.

"Pillow talk is fun," Kirsten says. "My last boyfriend lacked adjectives. You remember Rick, don't you Monica? I don't believe he ever said one adjective during the entire time we went out," she says laughing. "Your eyes, your lips, he labeled me like a biological diagram."

"Talk about dumb-as-a-box-of-rocks," laughs Monica. "I think it's special," I agree. "You never talk about your boyfriend, Tomas. Is he able to string sentences together or what?" asks Monica.

"Or is he like a chair? You know the type. He's like a piece of furniture. Where do I put the Tomas?" says Kirsten. "We've all had the big and wooden type."

"Yeah, you get a card and they're barely able to put an X at the bottom of it. It makes you wonder if they just bought it because of the way it looked. Pictures only baby, no words allowed," says Monica. "A coloring book is the last book the guy remembers picking up and reading."

"What about the reason we go out with them?" I ask. "Are we just as guilty because we fall for the box of Cracker Jacks and discard the prize? Some habits are hard to break. I fall for the package."

"But pillow talk," says Kirsten. "You two make me wish I had a boyfriend," whines Monica. "There's something so special about the words."

"The beauty of the words, that's what it's all about. My father got caught up in the beauty of the words," I say. I got caught up in the beauty of Tomas' words, I think.

When Tomas and I started going out, his words were the magic which unlocked the key to my heart. In the warmth of the summer nights, he explored and conquered the boundaries of my outlined existence. During the Los Angeles riots, in the midst of all that anger and violence, we played house in our own private world. The curfew fueling our passion. We lived in our own Camelot.

"Oh, Baby Bear, come out and see this," he said. "Oh Babycakes," I said. "It's beautiful. The colors are sub- liminal." I stood by him on the back porch. "It's practically the color of dried rose petals."

120

"Are you scared?" he asked. "A little," I admitted. "Don't be scared," he said. He wrapped his arm around my shoulder.

"The city's on fire, Babycakes," I said feeling a little anxious. "I'll protect you, always," he said. He held me firmly. "I believe it's my role on this earth."

"Do you think they'll get up here, I mean we are in Los Angeles, Babycakes," I said worried.

"Just look at the sky, kiddo. I've never seen such beauty rising above the city," he said. "You have to have all this destruction, just to get the beauty back in the city. Come inside, Baby Bear, before you get sick."

"I can't believe the city's got so much anger, it's such a beautiful city," I said.

"The city isn't angry," he said. "The people in the city are angry and that's the problem with this entire thing, this riot."

"But look at the sky," I said. I walked through the kitchen from the back porch into the front room. "Shall we watch the news, Babycakes?"

"Yes," he said. He turned on the television. "This is nice," I said. Of all the places in the city, this is the best place, I thought. Sitting warmly by his side on this old orange couch, the world can't touch me.

"This is where I belong," he said. "Look at those people on the television. They don't have a place. My place is with you. I'm here to protect you and to love you. I'll always take care of my Baby Bear."

"And you have a place, Babycakes," I said. I touched his warm thigh and I could feel an involuntary muscle spasm under his warm skin.

"Look at them crashing through the glass and metal, trying to even the score that they feel is so uneven. I firmly believe that if everyone found their place, then there wouldn't be so much anger," he said.

"Oh," I said. I looked into his black eyes, but I couldn't read his thoughts. When I looked at his face his mouth had a slight upward grin. "Why don't you turn off the television? I don't like watching all this destruction and unhappiness. It's not this way in the books."

"Poor little Sage, always reading someone else's words. You're lost in the books, just like your father was lost in the beauty of the words. You'll be all right, because Tomas is here to take care of you," he said.

"Will you, Tomas?" I asked. "Of course, I will," he said. "I feel better," I said comforted. "That's what I'm here to do. Don't be scared. I will always take care of you. There isn't anything in the world that can touch you as long as I am by your side. You're my role in life," he said.

"I'm tired," I said. "Baby Bear needs to get some sleep," he said. He kissed me on my forehead, just like an angel with soft warm mango lips. And I felt like I had entered into the pages of a perfect book.

"You don't need to walk, I'll carry you," he whispered into my right ear.

Tomas bent over and picked me up with those magnificent arms of his. This was as close to heaven as I get, I thought. I hung my head across his wide shoulders and inhaled his intoxicating scent of sweat and love. It was magical.

"I love you," I said whispering into his ear. The words needed to be said, I thought. I had never used them before.

"Let me get you to bed," he said. I believe he never heard those words, for he never registered the heat and passion I tried to convey with those innocent words.

The city was in turmoil and the windows remained open on that April night. He turned on the overhead light when he carried me into the bedroom, and in the harsh white glare and I looked at his face. His eyes were glazed as he slowly blinked with those fine black eyelashes.

I looked out the screen window. The night looked black as the artificial light cast a shadow against the ripped screen. A large moth kept flying into the screen. I watched the taupe colored animal continually fly into the screen. He tried to find a way out. His wings fluttered and his body filled with determination to get out of this house.

"Damn pest," Tomas said mechanically. "He doesn't mean any harm," I said. "Pest," he said. Tomas walked around the room. "What are you looking for?" I asked. "A magazine," he said. "Why?" I asked.

"I'm gonna kill it," he said. "Don't kill it," I pleaded. "Here we go," he said. Tomas ignored me as I sat on the bed. I watched him roll up the magazine, the pages turned uniformly. "Don't kill it, please, Tomas," I repeated. "Do you know what they do?" he asked. "I don't care what he does," I said.

"Shit, I missed him," he said. "Where did he go?" Tomas walked around the room. He looked like a soldier during a battle.

"Leave him alone," I begged. "Baby Bear, you don't know anything," he said, dismissively. "It's just an animal, a helpless animal," I pleaded.

"I'm gonna get him," he said. "There he is." Tomas jumped up on the bed, his black shoes trailed dirt on the clean white sheets.

"Don't," I screamed. I sat on the bed with my head on my lap as my hands covered my ears. "I don't want you to kill it!"

"Almost got him," he said. The moth flew into the corner of the room. "No, don't!" I screamed. Tomas lost his balance on the bed. The moth flew out of the corner and went to the overhead light with its white glass imprinted with flowers and leaves emanating warmth.

"Do you know what they do?" he asked. "It's just a helpless animal," I said. "Let me correct you and tell you it's an insect," he said. Tomas got off of the bed, and thumped on the hardwood floor. "He has his place in this world," I said. "Do you know what he'll do?" he asked. "I don't care, please don't hurt him," I begged. "You don't know what you're talking about, Sage," he said. "Now where did he go?" Tomas spun around the room, his head focused on the ceiling. "I don't see him, do you?"

"No, I don't," I said. I watched the shadows of fluttering wings against the light. I knew the moth was just trying to escape to the outside world.

"Listen, Sage. He'll feed upon clothing and that couch you have out in the front room. He'll gradually gnaw away at every- thing, until it's all ruined. That's what moths do," he said.

"Let him go," I said. "No, I can't," he said. "He'll ruin everything." "Please, don't," I pleaded. "There he is," he said. "I'll get him." The *moth tried to escape the big hands holding a magazine rolled up to kill. The moth flew to the window in an attempt to find the hole he had found once before.*

"Now I got him," Tomas said. He swung the magazine at the screen with all of his strength. He missed. I watched his tunnel vision fueled by anger.

"Where did he go?" he asked. "I'm not watching this. You're like a hunter going for the kill," I said.

"Don't be such a baby. You're too sensitive," he said. "There he is." Tomas jumped up on the bed and swung the magazine at the light. He hit the moth. I watched the body of the moth fall through the stale air of the room. The light brown carcass fell from grace and made a slight ping noise as it hit the floor.

"Got him," he said. Tomas smiled with his glazed black eyes. He sat on the bed and threw the magazine into a corner of the room. He bent over and picked up the carcass.

"He won't gnaw away at anything anymore," he said. "Doesn't he look helpless here in my fingers, poor bastard."

"You could have let him live. You could have caught him and let him go outside, it wouldn't have hurt you to do that," I said.

"Let it go, Sage," he said coldly. "Now, let me get rid of this thing." Tomas walked out of the room down the hallway. The toilet flushed. He returned to the room. The sink didn't turn on in the bathroom. I would have heard it. "Where were we?" he asked. Tomas sat on the bed. He pulled his shoes off without untying the laces. He delicately placed his trousers and shirt over the back of the chair.

"That's right. I'm putting my Baby Bear down to bed. The poor thing's tired and she needs her rest. Oh Baby Bear, you make me so happy," he said. Tomas shook the sheets to get the dirt off of them. The dirt fell onto the floor at the foot of the bed. "I'm tired, and I need to rest," I said. I crawled into the bed, slipping my shoes off but keeping my socks and clothing on.

"Now, what was the rule?" he asked. "Tomas, I'm really tired. What are you talking about?" I asked. "You know what I'm talking about. You have a brain. Don't you?" he asked. "Aren't you capable of logical thought?"

I looked at Tomas in his boxers, lying against my lace trimmed pillows. He looked so manly and strong. His arms were stretched behind his head, and the white sheet was pushed down by his feet. I admired the beautiful contours of his body and placed my hand on his warm stomach. His bristly black hair moved up and down as he breathed.

"No clothing in my bed," Tomas declared. "I'm just really tired, Tomas. Can't we break the rule, just this once?" I asked.

"You can't be a slacker, Baby Bear. Discipline is the key to the universe. Just peel off your clothes and I'll keep you warm. I promise I will. I won't let anything happen to you. You can trust me. Now be a good little girl and do as I say," he ordered.

"Yes, Tomas," I relented. I took off my sweats and T-shirt and climbed into bed with my bra and undies. My socks kept my feet warm. I pulled the sheet over my body and rested it under my neck.

"Everything," he said. "Yes, Tomas," I said. I took off the bra and underwear and threw them on the floor. I turned on my side away from him.

"Hey," he said. His feet touched my feet. I forgot I was still wearing my socks. "I forgot," I said. I reached down and pulled my socks off. I threw them on the floor.

"This is the way I like you," Tomas said. "Naked as the day you were born; this is the way you belong in my bed." "Yes," I said. I arranged the pillow under my head. "I want you over here," he said. He pulled me across the sheet as it rippled under my surprised body. I felt the warmth of his flesh and his locking embrace.

"Goodnight, Babycakes," I said. "Goodnight, Baby Bear," he said. I felt his hand move up and down and across the curve of my hip. The sheet separated me from his unwashed moth-kill- ing hand. I thought of the *moth and how in death, he had still achieved freedom.*

"I want to prove my love to you, tonight," he whispered in my ear.

"But, Tomas," I said.

He held his hand over my mouth. My words escaped unspoken. He whispered sweet adjectives into my ear. His kisses cleansed my body, like a whore's bath. He turned me over on my back and kissed every part of my body —except my rosy lips. I listened to the crickets sing outside the window. I watched his self-involved preoccupation with my body. The harsh bright overhead light backlit his face so I couldn't see any details of his features. He turned me over on my stomach and climbed on top of me. As he achieved the mighty role of king through his thrusts, I stared down the hallway dispassionately. For just one minute, I could see all of the ghosts in the house. The lace from the pillowcase stuck between my teeth, and his "Oh baby" was all that I felt and heard. A helicopter flew over us in the sky, and I could see the blue white spotlight as it shined through the windows in the bedroom. Ghetto birds.

"They're looking for criminals," he said as he climbed off of me.

"The riots," I said. I turned over and tightly held the sheet under my armpits and across my breasts.

"Do you want anything to drink? I'm thirsty. And I've got to let Steinbeck in before he cries outside," he said as he walked out of the room unclothed.

Steinbeck ran into the room and jumped up on the bed. He walked in circles until he found his place in the center. Tomas came back into the room and turned out the light. He crawled into bed and lay on his side.

"Come here," he said. "I'm fine," I said.

"Here, now," he ordered. Tomas pulled me across the bed and into his arms. His warm arms embraced me, holding me tightly and resting on the center of my chest.

"I can feel your heart beat, Baby Bear," he said. "Yes, you can," I said to the man who shared my sleep space. "I told you I will always be here for you and I mean it," he said. "I know you do, Babycakes," I said.

"Goodnight." "Goodnight Baby Bear, I love you," he said. For a moment, I was lost in the echoed silence. Then the sounds emerged. In the darkness of the night, the helicopters flew low over all of the unaffected areas. I listened to the bangs, bumps, and chops of the helicopter blades as it hovered across the sky. Then I placed my hand under my pillow and fell asleep grasping the page from The Pearl my father had given me so long ago.

"Intimacies of the bedroom," I say. "There is nothing as special as the sweet words spoken between two people behind the bedroom door."

"The best part of the relationship," agrees Monica. "The best part is those soft words spoken."

"I always love the bedroom," says Kirsten. "That's the easy part. It's outside the bedroom where the living is hard. In the bedroom, there is a desperate isolation among the sheets. Outside the bedroom, control becomes the issue."

"You two really think that?" I ask. *I wish I had that philosophy, I thought.*

"Except for the last guy I went out with. That was miserable. I got sucked in and I didn't have any fun. You know one of those situations where you're sorry, but you're just obliged to get an- other number down on your score card," laughs Monica. "He wanted to save me. What nonsense, I don't need to be saved."

"You didn't tell me about him," says Kirsten. "The Rapunzel complex, huh?"

"Yes, I did," Monica says. "Dog man, you remember him. He wanted me to let my hair down. He said he could save me if I let down my boundaries."

"You guys," I say. *Tomas and his theories are everywhere, I thought.*

"They talk about us this way and don't have any guilt. We're so diseased. We have to be guiltless," says Monica. "I always turn my head at a good-looking man, and there are no age limits. Sometimes men can be so sexy with grey hair. But anyway, Kirsten, don't you remember this guy?"

"Is this the one you gave that line to?" Kirsten asks. "Yes, this is line man," Monica confirms with a nod. "What line?" I ask. I like to be included in my peer group, I thought.

"Are you done yet?" asks Monica. "That was the line. You know, with condoms you can't always be sure." Monica laughs. "You guys are awful," I say laughing too. "You're my kind of women. Are you done yet? I love that. I have to remember that." "Monica is awful. We love her, but she's bad. She's a keeper," says Kirsten. "Are you ready, Monica? I've got to get back to work." "And I've got to go riding. So is the life of a commissioned employee," says Monica.
Tara Botel Doherty

"She's really enjoying this," says Kirsten. "We'll see you later, Sage."

"Don't work so hard, Sage," says Monica. Monica and Kirsten stand up and walk away. They turn and wave as they walk out the door. I am left alone with my thoughts, fears, and memories.

Fifteen

I LOVE CHINESE FOOD. *The aroma of the eastern spices, ginger and chili powder escaping from the white take-out containers. The glazed, sweet, sugared pineapple and green peppers, bathed in the hot pink sauce. The greasy taste of the hot and sour soup, as it goes down your throat numbing your taste buds. Gummy bits of sticky white rice covered in soy sauce spill onto the plate.*

Tomas knows I love Chinese food. Last week when I got home from work, he had Chinese food waiting for me. He bought moo shu pork, with the pancakes and plum sauce on the side; sweet and sour pork, broccoli beef, chow mein, and both steamed and fried rice.

"I know what you need," he said self-assured.

"Yes, you do," I said. And no you don't, I thought. "I'll take care of you, have a seat," he directed. I sat at the table, with the old vinyl tablecloth. There were certain spots which were worn away from age.

"Let me get you a plate," he said. He walked to the cabinet above the sink. Tomas knew where everything was, because he rearranged the entire house and its contents. I never bothered knowing where things were in this house. If I needed something, I looked for it. It was never that important for me to know the whereabouts of inanimate objects. If I looked hard enough and prayed to Saint Anthony, things would appear. I never questioned it.

"A plate," I said. "Yes, a plate," he said. "But half of the fun is

129

eating out of the cartons," I said. "You're not a child, anymore," he said in an insipid tone. "Yes, Tomas," I said. But the cartons are the fun, I thought. "Here you go," he said. "Let me get that for you, I'll fill your plate. I know how much you need."

"Yes, Tomas," I agreed. I've been a child all my life in this kitchen. The warmest and most comforting room in this house refuses to let me grow up. I see the ghosts in the refrigerator dated from the Fifties, with the chunked ice keeping the freezer door closed and inaccessible. Opening it up with its unlit contents and chrome pull out handle, I see the past.

Hot nights when I can't sleep, I pull a chair to the refrigerator and sit in front of it, pulling the door open and absorbing the chill. The motor hums and the fan belts rattle. I sit and feel the cold, because at least that means I can feel something. I close my eyes tightly, fold my hands and say a Hail Mary because it's so much easier on the tongue than the Our Father. I say my prayer accompanied by the musical hum and belch of the refrigerator. I see the pots and pans and death platters which have filled this insulated cube. I see the deviled eggs and relish trays that were brought on crystal after Rose of Sharon was buried. After my father's wake noodle casseroles and onion dip sat in there until they grew a green fuzzy mold and were finally thrown away. When my grandmother died, I was alone. All the family friends had been buried for years.

And then it appears, the pot of vegetable soup. When I close my eyes I am taken back to what seemed to me like a magical night—making vegetable soup with my mother. Rose of Sharon had been her favorite, but this time I got to spend time with Mom in the kitchen. I was so thrilled. I never knew that she was broken from the loss of Rose of Sharon. In this kitchen, I was a child. She was my teacher. I think of that night and how I stirred that soup until there was no broth left in the pot. There were only slimy, mushy vegetables, overcooked past any flavor. The bottom of the pot, burned and blackened. My grandmother made me go to sleep that night, despite my screaming and yelling. I wouldn't let her throw out the pot of soup. It stayed in the refrigerator until the smell was so bad, it infested *everything else in the refrigerator. We were never able to use that pot again, because the enamelware cracked from Grandma's scrubbing it. It was destined for the trash heap with that blackened bottom.*

"I think that's enough food for you," he said.

"Yes, sir," I agreed. What irony, I thought. The things that drew us together become old and repetitive, practically smothering. Early in the relationship I thought his caretaking was sweet; now I feel as if I've gotten a mother. I'm suffocating.

"If you want more, you can have it later," he instructed. The refrigerator inhaled and exhaled with mechanical of white noise. Steinbeck scratched at the back door. He smelled the food through the open window and knew I would give him food if he was at my feet. I looked across the table at Tomas. He cut the sweet and sour pieces with the side of his fork, instead of using a knife. We ate in silence.

"How was your day, Babycakes?" I asked. "You better eat your food, it's getting cold. That's all you're getting," he announced.

"Yes, Tomas," I agreed. It wasn't that long ago that things were much different, I thought. I had become used to eating cold food. We would spend so much time talking. The food would become ice cold and it didn't bother me.

"I have a surprise for you," he said. "What is it?" I asked. "It wouldn't be a surprise if I told you," he said sternly. "Yes, sir," I said. I cut apart the chow mein noodles and mushed them into the plate. "Steinbeck has to go to the vet."

"Why?" he asked.

"He's got a hot spot," I said. "Jesus Christ," he said raising his voice. "Do you have to talk about this while we're eating? It's disgusting. You made me lose my appetite." He threw his fork on the plate, pushed back the chair, and walked out of the kitchen.

I took a deep breath and stayed in my chair. I'm not going to come after you and apologize, I thought.

Steinbeck scratched at the door. His whiny cries persist. I walked to the back door and let him inside.

"It's all right, baby," I said. Steinbeck looked at me with his begging eyes. "Here you go," I said. I placed my plate on the floor. Steinbeck wagged his tail as he gobbled up the scraps. "Do you have to feed him off of our plates?" Tomas asked. He stood in the doorway of the kitchen.

"I'll wash the plate. He wants to feel included. Steinbeck's a big baby, aren't you?" I said. I touched his coat.

"I'm going to bed," he said. "I'm gonna stay up, do you mind?" I asked. "Do you want the surprise?" he asked. "It'll be in the bedroom with me."

"I'll be there in a minute," I said. "I want to do the dishes and feed Steinbeck. It won't take me more than twenty minutes."

"Hurry up," he said. "And don't read your book tonight. You need to deal with reality."

Tomas walked out of the doorway and disappeared. "Steinbeck, how about some dog chow?" I picked up the bag and poured it on the plate. I sat at the table fingering the tablecloth with small circular motions. After Steinbeck inhaled his food, he scratched at the back door. I stood up and let him out. As I walked back in the kitchen, I picked up the plate off the floor. I slid it in the sink and turned on the hot water. Standing over the sink at the window, I could smell the night blooming jasmine and tea roses in the garden. Steam from the hot water rose out of the sink and made me perspire. I placed my hands in the water and it burnt them. I readjusted the faucet and felt the warm water.

I washed the dishes with circular strokes, the way my grandmother taught me. Only two dishes and four pieces of cutlery, and the dishes were done. I sat at the table and opened the book. Yellowed vines trailed the loose pages of Cannery Row. In the silence, I secretly wished for things to be the way they used to be. But wishes are like church candles, they're only as good as they burn. I closed the book and said a prayer. I had delayed as long as I could. I turned out the light, and walked into the bedroom.

The room was lit with flickering candles. Tomas lay on the bed naked with his left-hand propping up his head on the pillow. A big brown bag rested on my pillow.

"I've been waiting for you, Baby Bear," he said. "Here I am, Tomas," I said. "Come here," he whispered. I sat on the bed and let him pull me close to him. My feet dangled off of the bed as he kissed me on the forehead.

"You know the rule," he said. "Yes, Tomas," I said. I stood up and obligingly peeled off every piece of clothing from my body. This was becoming a desensitizing chore, I thought. I got into bed.

"Watch out, you'll break them," he said. "What is it?" I asked. "I wanted to apologize for last week," he said. "I didn't mean it. You made me so mad. I ripped up the book, because you made me so mad. I wanted you to pay attention to me, and not the stupid book. I care about you so much, Sage. You'll always be my Baby Bear."

"I know you didn't mean it," I said. My father's copy of Cannery Row rests atop the counter fragmented.

"You made me so mad. I just reacted." "I know," I said. "I care about you," he said. He leaned into me and hugged me. I felt tears stream down his eyes and fall on my shoulders

"I know, I know," I said. I listened to his quiet sobbing. I was torn by the dark, rain-filled clouds, I thought.

"Look in the bag," he said separating our bodies. "Here." "My favorite," I said. "How thoughtful of you. It was very sweet. You know how much I love fortune cookies."

"I got a dozen, just for the two of us. Sit next to me, Baby Bear," he said. "I want you next to me."

"Yes, Tomas," I said. We sat propped up against the headboard with pillows. The sheet rested on our stomachs. We sat side by side. Tomas creased the sheet against his body, sheltering his nakedness from me. I noticed.

"You know the rules," he said. "Yes, Tomas," I said. "You do remember," he said. "We count to three, and on number three we crack open the cookie."

133

"Should we dump them?" I asked. "Why not," he said as he emptied the bag on the white sheet. "Which one do I want?"

"Only touch the one you're gonna take, you can't touch the rest," I said.

"My superstitious, little Baby Bear," he said. He touched my hair and ran his hand down it. "I'll take this one."

"Let me pick mine, I have to see which one speaks to me," I said. "I think this one has my vibe."

"My little SNAG, let's count to three. Remember on three. One. Two. Three, go," he said. "What does yours say?"

"What does SNAG mean?" I asked. "Don't be so sensitive. A SNAG is an acronym for sensitive, new age gal. That is what you are with your metaphysical, in- cense burning, karmic self, isn't it?" he asked.

"Yes, Tomas," I said. "My fortune says, 'You have an active mind and a keen imagination.' That sounds like me."

"'Good sense is the master of human life.' I don't like this one. This one doesn't sound like me, what a rip," he said. "Let's go again. I have to listen to my vibe, and it should lead me to the right fortune. Right?"

"I'll take this one, it speaks to me," I said. "This one speaks to me, it's gonna be great. One. Two. Three, break. What is this, what a rip off," he said.

"What does it say?" I asked. "'Adjust finances, make budgets, to improve your standing.'"

"That's not bad, Tomas. Mine said 'You have an active mind and a keen imagination'," I said.

"That one should have been mine," he said. "That fortune sounds more like me. Let's try this again. One. Two. Three, break. This is bullshit. I don't believe this crap. We must always have old memories and young hopes.' What a crock. I'm getting really pissed off."

"You didn't wait for me, but my fortune cookie said 'You will make many changes before settling satisfactorily,'" I said.

"Now see, that one was for me. You're always gonna be a waitress.

134

You're lost in the beauty of the words, just like your father. Sage, you'll be there until you retire because you're comfortable. You're never gonna use your college degree. And don't even get me started on your jewelry making. That jewelry was stupid and no one would buy it. What an idiotic idea," he said.

"Don't be so mean, Tomas. They're only fortune cookies. It's not like it's a matter of life and death, black and white. Lighten up," I said.

"Don't tell me how to feel, Sage. You're not me, and you don't know exactly how I feel. You may think you do because you're a know it all, but you don't," he snarled.

"I don't want to play this anymore," I said. I started to get up from the bed.

"You're not going anywhere, not until we finish the game, Sage," he snapped. He grabbed my wrist and squeezed it until I had no feeling in it.

"Next cookie," I said. I massaged my wrist with my fingers and stared into his black eyes.

"One. Two. Three, go," he said as he crushed the cookie with one hand. 'What a crock, again. The only way to have a friend is to be one.' They ripped me off. Those bastards ripped me off."
"Calm down, Tomas," I said.

"What does your fortune say?" he asked. "I don't want to read it. I told you I wanted to stop this, and you didn't listen to me. Please stop, Tomas," I said.

"Read it," he snipped. He grabbed my wrist, squeezing it tighter. "I'm gonna keep squeezing until you read."

"Please stop," I begged. "Read it," he snarled. "Read it or you'll lose your hand. Isn't this your writing hand? Don't you need it to take orders at work?"

"'You will be fortunate in the opportunities presented to you.' That's what it says, Tomas," I said. "Please let go of my wrist."

"I want that one," he said. He dropped my wrist. "That one should be mine, I was gonna choose it, but you touched it. I want it."

135

As I dropped the fortune, Tomas lunged for me and shoved me out of the bed. I hit the hardwood floor. I felt the dirt and gravel against my bare flesh on the floor.

"Oh, Baby Bear, what happened?" he said. He hung off of the bed over me.

"I fell," I said. You shoved me, I thought. "Are you all right?" he asked. He towered over me. "Let me help you up, Baby Bear."

"No, I can get up on my own. Give me a minute. I'll be all right. I'm lucky I'm not as bony as I used to be," I said in forced laughter.

"Come up here and let me fix the broken Baby Bear," he said. He patted his hand on the sheet. "Come on now, I'll fix you."

I got off the floor and into the bed. I felt his violent arms curl around me, as I attempted to move away from him.

"I'm sorry, Baby Bear," he said.

He kissed the back of my neck with abrasive tooth-filled kisses. "I know you're sorry, Tomas. I know," I said. I fell asleep with the pain, and woke up to the black and blue bruises on my wrist and the side of my body.

"Do you want to go take a smoke break, Sage?" asks Matty sneaking up on me in my own private memory. "You look like you need one."

"Yeah, sure. I won't be long," I say. I walk out the swinging door, and through the working kitchen.

"Hey, kiddo," Freddy says. "Hey, Freddy," I say. One of the worst aspects of working in a restaurant is the continual salutations and thanking every two-legged creature you encounter, I thought.

I keep walking and go up the stairs, swinging the screen door open with one push. I walk to the catering tables and sit on the only chair. The blue padding of the chair is split just below my crotch, and I stare down and watch the spongy filling escape.

"Momma's here, baby. My head is spinning. We've so many orders, and Miss Lee and I are arguing. And it's not even something I did. The Perfect One rearranged the files and then took an order without calling back to verify. That Lulu couldn't find her ass with both hands," Jo said in one breath.

"Oh, Jo," I say. "What can Momma do to put a smile on that pretty face?" she asks.

"I wish it was that easy. It's everything. I don't even feel like I'm here today. I feel so mechanical," I say.

"Momma says that you're not a lifer. You'll get out of here one day, but don't let those old bitches get to you," she says. "Where are my cigarettes?"

"Here, have one of mine," I say. I hand her a cigarette. "Here". I light a match as she puts the cigarette into the flame.

"Is that it?" Jo asks. "What do you mean?" I ask. "It's not my place to say anything, but boy trouble is the problem, isn't it?" she asks.

"What makes you think that?" I ask. "I saw the bruise on your wrist last week and the way you walked," she says. "Everyone saw it, but no one said anything. We all thought you were too smart for it to be the obvious thing."

"Jo, what do you know about love?" I ask. "I know I've had five husbands. Two of them beat the shit out of me, but honey that was before we ever knew that it wasn't right. Things are different today," she says taking a drag off of her cigarette and moving the smoke with her other hand when she exhales.

I look at this little woman who had sold herself short her en- tire life and had laughed at telling me she was an easy lay when she was my age. At bars, when anyone dared her, she gave away her womanliness for free. That's a very sad life, I thought.

"I know, Jo. But..." I explain. "I don't want to hear about

butts. Everyone has one. There is no excuse. It only has to happen once and that is one too many times. Baby, wake up and smell the roses. I know you've been with this guy a long time. There are no excuses," she explains through exhaled smoke.

"Jo, I don't know," I say. "Honey, all those men that I married are dead, all five of them. And the only one who was decent to me was Pauly, and I loved him as much as I could love at that point in my life. The bastard gave me fifteen wonderful years where I didn't have to work and bought me the house. He never laid a hand on me. And that is the way it should be," Jo says.

"Jo, I'm confused". "You've got your loins talking and not your brain," she replies.

"It's not that easy," I whine. "The last time you didn't make any excuses. My favorite time was the dog excuse. Let me remember it. Oh, yeah, the dog jumped on you and hit you in the face. That one was a keeper, Sage," she says.

"You didn't say anything, Jo," I say. "I'm your friend, honey. I'm not your mother. The one before Pauly would kick me around like a card table. You know when you kick the legs of a card table to set them straight. I didn't know better, you do," she says.

"Well, he didn't mean it," I say. "Don't make excuses, or you'll talk yourself into believing that you deserve this kind of treatment. I can't remember if it was number two, or was it number three? I would work my ass off cocktailing and this asshole sat at home. When I didn't get home early enough, he told me I was out whoring. He would hit me in my face, because he knew that was how I made the money. Thank God for that Max Factor pancake make-up. Get out. I'm not gonna share any more of my shit with you. You're a smart one and you'll figure it all out. I know you will, I have faith in you," she says. Jo bends over and hugs me.

"You're a winner," she whispers in my ear. "Thanks, Jo," I say. "I can feel Miss Lee talking about me. My ears are burning. I better go. And pick up your butts; I'm tired of doing it. Now that was the mother in me," she says. Jo disappears down the stairs and waves her hands in the air like the crazy woman she is.

I put my head on the table and I feel as if my life is spinning before my eyes on a television screen. I stare at the plastic baggies for catered lunches. They are filled with salt, pepper and sugar. The same kind of plastic knives and forks that my mother was furiously cleaning with the paper napkin when she sat at the park table decades ago trying to wipe away the fears.

"Hey kiddo, are you all right?" Jose asks. "I'll be all right," I say. "Have you gotten back to the jewelry? That was some of the most beautiful and creative jewelry I have ever seen," he says.

"I'm thinking about it," I say. I stopped making jewelry when I met Tomas. He laughed at it and called it silly. I remember he told me not to quit my day job. I didn't listen with my ears, I listened with my heart, I think.

"You've got a gift," he says. He walks away. One of the nicest men in the world, works for a minimum wage. He is a childless man with sore legs and a love for new experiences that I have never seen before. I like to think my father would have been like him, if he had found the beauty not only in words, but also in real life. I like to think that my father would have had the gentle disposition of this man.

"Bye, Jose, I better get back. They'll get mad at me and start talking about me," I say.

"Kiddo, they'll always talk about you. It's in their nature," he says laughing while he holds the knife carving roses out of radishes.

Sixteen

I TURN AROUND AND walk through the door, holding the rusted pipe handrail as I make my way down the slippery mopped floor. Smelling the chocolate rugala, I walk to the grease stained steel ovens, and the rack resting next to them. On a tray, I spot the warm chocolate wrapped in buttery dough and topped with large granules of sugar. They smell heavenly. I pick up an end piece and look around the kitchen. I put the piece in my mouth and close my eyes to the ecstasy of this delicate morsel. I take three more pieces and put them in my pocket, leaving an obvious void on the browned baking paper. I walk through the kitchen and out of the swinging door to the waitresses' area.

"How are you doing, now?" asks Cherry. She sits at the back table continually stirring her coffee.

"I'm fine," I say. But not really, I think. "You know if you need anything," she says, moving her head up and down. "You can always talk to me, Sage."

"I know," I say. She stares down in her coffee cup. I smile. Cherry has her own clouds that roll in and sit on the mountain range. The clouds are everywhere, I think. "There you are," says Matty. "Here I am," I say. "I sent Micky out for you," Matty says wiping crumbs off of her already smeared orange lipstick.

"I'm here," I say. "That was really long for a short break," she says coldly. "Sorry," I say. "Are you really? You know there has to be one waitress on the floor at all times," she says.

Matty stands in front of me itching her scalp with a pen. I listen to the abrasive sound and watch the flakes fall on her collar.

"You are the waitress on the floor," I say. "This is a round robin. Let's drop it, all right?"

"Watch the floor, I have to go get my pills. My back is going out on me, again," she says walking away. "You have two call parties. I got them both coffee. They're on tables thirteen and eight." Matty disappears through the kitchen and runs to the toilet.

I walk out on the floor and look at the numbers on the table legs. I approach table thirteen and look at the young woman sitting at the table. She looks vaguely familiar.

"Sagey!" She screams.

"Rosemary," I say. She stands and I hug her. Rosemary seems shorter than I remember her. She has a slim figure.

"You look so grown up," I say standing away from her. "So do you. You look great," she says. "How long has it been?" "It's been more than five years, I think. The years all mesh together after a while. I don't know where they went," I say.

"Do you remember these?", she says pointing to her ears. I look at her earrings. Silver wire wrapped around broken glass shards. My graduation present to her. I worked on those for weeks wrapping the glass, and braiding the wire. I wanted them to be delicate, but dangerous. "How did you find me?" I ask. "I was visiting my mom; you know she still lives in the old neighborhood, don't you?" she asks.

"No, I didn't," I say. "I heard about your grandmother. I'm

sorry," she says. "That was a long time ago," I say. "It doesn't really bother me anymore. Death seems like something that just happens."

"I was visiting my mom, and she didn't know if you were still at the house. I left a note on the door about a week ago, but I never heard anything from you. I talked to a nice-looking guy. He said he would pass along the note. I've been here for a week. I'm on my way home today," she says.

"That was Tomas, my boyfriend. He didn't tell me you had stopped by, or else I would have called you," I say.

"Sagey, I just thought you were too busy," she says. "Rosemary, I'm never too busy for you," I say. "But how did you find me?"

"The newspaper," Rosemary says. "The newspaper?" I ask. "The review for this place, it had your picture in it," she says. "That's right, Fine Dining reviewed us. Miss Lee and Lulu insisted I be in the picture. I didn't know it had come out yet. I didn't want to be in it," I admit.

"I didn't have to look at the name. I saw you. Those eyes of yours, they never change. You look like the same little girl, only grown up now," she says.

"Rosemary, it's so good to see you," I say warmly. "What have you been doing?"

"I'm on my way back home. I live in the Bay Area and I've got an eighteen-month little baby girl," she says. "But I've really got to go. I wanted to talk to you about the earrings. Do you still make your jewelry? I always get compliments on these earrings, and I wanted to know if you'd be interested in making more?" asks Rosemary.

"I haven't done it in years," I say. "Would you be interested in doing it again?" she asks. "I don't know. There's a lot going on right now," I say. "Sagey, you don't have to give me any answers right now. I am glad I got to see you, I've missed you," she says.

"Rosemary, do you really have to leave? I get off of work in a few hours. You can't stick around until then?" I ask.

"Here is my card; you can always call me. Actually, I want to talk to you about your jewelry. I have an offer for you. So, you'd better call me. And my mother would love to see you. She sends her big fat kisses. Don't be a stranger, Sagey," she says. "I love you like a sister."

"I know you do," I say. I remember the big fat kisses my mom would give Rose-of-Sharon, my kisses were always sloppy.

Rosemary stands up, and hugs me with her trim, petite arms. "Goodbye, Sagey," she says.   Rosemary walks out the door. I watch her walk across the windows and out of sight. I look around the deli and behind the counters. I see Lulu. She looks at me.

"Now that you're done visiting, do you know you have another table?" she asks in a flat tone.

"I forgot," I say shrugging my shoulders. "Come here," Lulu says. "Yes," I say. I walk over to where she stands. I look at Lulu with her crisp white blouse buttoned up to her neck. Her black short haircut a half inch too short, Betty Page Style, on her forehead, making her look like a teenager.

"You have another table. If you don't like the job, quit. Waitresses grow on trees and don't forget that," she threatens.

"Yes, ma'am," I spit the words out and walk away. "Come back here," she orders. "After your shift, we're going into the office. You think you're so special," she says wagging her tiny finger at me.

I look at the nail-bitten edges of her finger nail. "Don't make this personal," I say. "You don't follow the rules," she

144

says. "If you don't like it, quit." I feel the anger boiling inside of me. I always listen to Lulu and take it.

"Today is not the day to do this," I say. "Is this one of your sensitive days? I don't have time for you and your craziness," she barks.

"Peter is the manager. You are not. If you have a problem with me, we'll take it up with him. I'm going to go and do my job, is that all right with you?" I ask.

"Go," she says as she turns around and walks away. I stand with my face red in anger and I can feel my heart racing. The fast thumps in my chest and the heat in my face make me hot. I sit in a chair for a minute, to catch my breath.

Rosemary was as close as a sister to me. She was my only childhood friend. Grandma would let me go and play after school at her house. But I was forbidden to eat dinner or sleep over at her house. Rosemary's mother would make us afternoon snacks. In the bright orange of their kitchen, we would sit at the table and pretend like we were grown-ups at a restaurant.

"You're so lucky," I said. "What are you talking about?" Rosemary asked. "Girls, go and wash your hands before you eat," said Rose-mary's mother.

"They're clean, Mom," Rosemary pleaded. "Go," she said. I followed Rosemary into the bathroom. We washed our hands in the petal pink of the bathroom. When she finished rinsing her hands, I washed away the dirt after she was done. I followed her back into the kitchen and sat next to her.

"One more minute, girls," her mother said. Her mother stood at the sink. I smelled the sweetness of sliced oranges. Her mother turned toward us and placed two plates on the table. One plate had sliced oranges and the other had graham crackers.

"Here you go, girls," she said. "Thanks, Mom," said Rosemary. "Thanks," I said. "What do you mean I'm lucky?" Rosemary asked. "Excuse me, Mommy. Can we get something to drink?"

145

"Listen kiddo," Rosemary's mother said. "Do you want milk or water?" she asked.

"We'll have milk, please," Rosemary said. Rosemary always answered for me. Her mother put two glasses of milk on the table, and then kissed Rosemary on the top of her head.

"Don't do that, Mom," Rosemary said. "I'm sorry. I forgot that you're all grown up now," her mother said.

Her mother stood at the sink. She washed dishes. "You're lucky," I said. I could feel my milk moustache on my top lip.

"I don't get it, Sage," she said. "You have a mom," I said. We ate our graham crackers and orange slices. "You're crazy," Rosemary said. I put my half-eaten graham cracker down on the plate, and I stood up.

"I have to leave. I'll see you tomorrow at school, Rosemary," I said. I picked up my bag and walked out of the door.

"What happened?" asked Rosemary. I heard her voice question me as I closed the front door.

Rosemary never said anything about that afternoon. We pretended like it never happened. When other kids teased me at school and called me crazy, Rosemary protected me.

Seventeen

I WALK OVER TO table eight feeling Lulu's gaze.

"Hello. I'm sorry for keeping you. Can I help you?" I ask. I look at the customer with the empty coffee cup and lotus pink lips.

"Hello, Sage," whispers my mother. "What do you want?" I ask. "I wanted to see you," she says. I look at her and she is not what I expected. I have her hair and lips, but I would never wear pink lipstick. Other than blood and her biological necessity as my mother, there is a strange familiarity about her.

"What do you want for breakfast?" I inquire coldly. "I understand your coldness. Lox and cream cheese, please, Sage," she says.

"What kind of bagel? Onion, egg, or water bagel, which one do you want?" I ask.

"An onion bagel," she says flatly. "Toasted?" I ask. "Yes, please, little one," she begs with a timid voice. "Thanks," I say blankly and walk away from the table. I walk into the kitchen and I feel all of the blood drain from my face. I put the order up and my hand shakes.

"Are you all right, Sage?" Matty asks. "Wonderful," I reply. "You look pale. Have you had anything to eat?" she asks like a mother.

147

"Matty, finish this table for me. You can keep the tip. I feel sick to my stomach. I've got to go in the back. I can't be here right now. Please do this for me, I'll make it up to you," I say.

"No problem, go outside and get some air," she says. "Thanks," I say. I walk through the kitchen and everything is a blur. I run up the back stairs, through the door, and past the catering tables and stand in the alley.

It wasn't what I thought it would be. She wasn't the way I thought she would be. I expected her to be broken and sickly.

When I was ten, I ran away from my grandmother's house. I celebrated my birthday in November, in an uncelebrated manner. It was the day I decided I could find my mother. I felt she could save me. I didn't ask permission to leave. I just opened the door and walked away.

I walked over the tall hill of Montana Street watching the homes filled with happy people. Windows were open and other kids played with their balls and bats in their front yards. I crossed at the light and walked down to Sunset Boulevard. I was going to get bread for the table like my mother. This was the last place I knew my mother had been.

I walked into the store and went over to the bread aisle. I thought I could find her there, but my mother was not there.

"Do you need help, little one?" a woman asked me. "No," I said. I played with the buttons on my fuzzy purple coat with the vinyl sash.

"Are you here with someone?" she asked. "No," I answered. "What are you looking for?" she asked. "Maybe I can help." "No, I don't think so. I'm not supposed to talk to strangers," I said.

"You don't recognize me?" she asked. "No," I said. I looked at her. She had a red polyester shirt on that came to the bottom of her hips. It was untucked hanging over a black pair of trousers. She had a black apron tied at her waist.

"I live down the street from you. My house is the pink and white house in the next block. The pink geraniums in the window box and the pink mailbox," she said.

148

"No, well maybe," I said.

I look at her name tag, and it said Mrs. Webster.

"I know your grandmother. She's a very different woman. When the Santa Ana's blow I can smell the sweet perfume of her roses all the way up to my house. Does she know that you're here by yourself?" she asked.

"No," I said. "It's a big place for a little girl to be by herself. If you wait a few minutes, I'll give you a ride home. My shift is almost over," she said.

"I don't know," I said. "You think about it. I'll swing by here when I get off and see if you're still around," she said and smiled. "Yes, ma'am. I'll think about it," I said. I walked the bread aisle and felt close to my mother. I remembered her perfect hair and pink lips. I looked at the plastic bags filled with bread. They were labeled with adjectives like new and improved. No sugar added remained in my mind.

"Little one, do you need a ride?" asked the woman. She walked up behind me.

"I don't know. I should probably walk. I don't know who you are, you know," I said.

"I think it's all right," she said. "I'll talk to your grandmother, so she doesn't get mad at you."

"Well all right, I guess so," I said. "Follow me, little one," she said. I walked behind her and looked at the double knot tied on the back of her apron.

"Here we go," she said. I stood in front of a black VW Bug. It had orange and pink, and green and blue flowers stuck all over the body.

"A nice car," I said. "I like it; it suits me," she said. The car sounded as loud as a meat grinder and she drove staring straight ahead at the road. We got down the hill and I saw my grandmother with a worried look on her face.

"Sage, where have you been?" she asked when I got out of the car.

"I went to the store," I said. "Go inside the house," she screamed. "Why?" I asked. "Because I said so," she said. She pointed to the house.

"Yes, Grandma," I said. "Now," she said. "Yes, Grandma," I said. I walked into the house. Through the glass, I watched my grandmother lean into the window of the little black car. My grandmother was angry and screamed at the woman. The woman pulled out of the driveway and drove down the street. My grandmother shook her fist and screamed wild, angry words.

Whenever I sold candy every year at school, my grand-mother walked with me through the neighborhood. She never allowed me to knock on the door of the house with the white window boxes filled with pink geraniums. When I rode my bike down the street, I would wave at the neighbor lady who gave me a ride home. While I was at camp that summer, the lady moved away.

I put out the cigarette in the broken gravel of the alley. I watch a woman hold her little daughter over the garbage bin of the five and dime. The little girl fishes out a broken doll and a fry- ing pan with a broken handle. They both have the same old blue eyes. I walk back into the restaurant, to the woman who shares my blood, and called me "little one" decades ago.

"Bad call, Sage. She left a fin. A very good tip for a single woman," said Matty. She holds the five up to my face.

"She left?" I ask. "I told her you went on your break. She didn't touch her lox. When she heard you were gone, she got up and walked out of the restaurant," says Matty.

I run out of the restaurant and look down the street. The sky is clear and there is no sign of her anywhere.

"Is everything all right, baby doll?" asks Jo. She stands on the concrete sidewalk in the doorway.

"Yes, it's fine, Jo," I say. "Then why are you standing out there?" she asks. "I forgot something," I say. "Come inside, baby doll. I don't want Lulu to see you out here. She doesn't need any more ammunition than she already has on you," says Jo. She puts her arm around me and pushes me back into the restaurant.

"I know," I say. I walk back in the restaurant. My fingers and my body feel numb. Time sleeps and the day moves slowly. Faces look blank and I've lost the music of this job. I wish the work day would end. I look at the slow-moving clock, teasing me with its large arms.

"Sage, you don't look like you're having any fun," says Cherry. "One hour left and then I can go to the cemetery," I say. "Who's at the cemetery?" Cherry asks. "It's the anniversary of my father's death," I say. "I'm sorry," Cherry says. "Don't be," I say. "It was a long time ago." "Well, I am," she said.

I walk away. Roses are what my grandmother would want, I think. I stand over the sink in the back kitchen and scrub my mustards. EVERY DAY THE MUSTARDS MUST BE CLEANED THOROUGHLY. I pour the regular mustard in the cleaned jars and slop it on the side of one. I wipe it off with my hand and pour the horseradish-laced mustard into the jars. I can feel the horseradish rise up and try to slap sense into me. I can feel the tears beginning.

"They were looking for you, Sage," says Cherry. "Who?" I ask. "Someone in the deli," she says. "More shit, just what I needed today," I say. "Cherry can you watch my station, I'm gonna go over and see what they want." "No problem, Sage. If someone gets seated in your station, I'll write it on a piece of paper," Cherry says.

"Keep it," I say. I walk through the door of a long corridor and into the back office. It's really a cubby hole with a desk, but they call it an office.

"Who wants me?" I ask. Peter and Lulu are talking and sitting in chairs. Peter looks at me and Lulu smiles at me.

"Sage, we need to talk," says Peter. "Yes, Peter," I say. "Excuse me," says Lulu. I see the smile on her round face as

151

she walks past me and out to the deli.

"Sage, Lulu said you're showing her no respect. She is the assistant manager, and Miss Lee's niece. We can't have renegades out on the floor," he says.

"Yes, Peter," I say.

"What can we do about this?" he asks with a fatherly tone. "I don't know," I say. "I think you need some time off," he says. "I'm off for the next two days," I say. "Take off the entire week," he says. "I think you need time to clean out your closet and get things in order."

"A whole week?" I ask. "It's only a week. I've talked to the other girls and they'll cover you. You just need to relax and get happy," he says.

"Yeah, sure," I say. I stand up and walk away. "Don't do that," he screams out at me. "Give me a break," I say. I walk away and shake my hand at him. "You've got five minutes on the floor," says Matty. She sits on a chair eating a bowl of soup and a bagel.

"So do you," I say. "Don't worry about me. I'm covered. You should be worrying about yourself," Matty says. As she chews the food, the plate from her dentures shifts restlessly in her mouth.

"Yeah, worry about yourself," laughs Bertha. She crams potato chips into her face with her long, dragon nails.

"Old bitches," I say under my breath. "Don't let them get to you, Sage. You're just having a bad day, that's all it is," Cherry says.

"I don't need this," I say. "You're not a lifer," she says. "This is all they have. They don't have anything outside of this."

"I don't feel sorry for them. They get what they deserve," I say in an aggravated tone.

"Relax on your days off and don't think about them," she says.

"I have a week off. And those two bitches knew about it. They're gonna work my shift. Lulu complained about me," I say. "Baby doll, didn't you hear me call for you? I've been looking all over for you," Jo says as she walks up to me.

"No, I didn't know you were the one calling for me," I say. "Baby doll, I forgot this in my pocket," Jo says. She hands me a piece of paper. "It was the funniest thing. This woman paid the bill and began to walk out of the door. Matty called out bread for the table and the woman turned around. She wrote this note and asked me to give it to you."

"Thanks, Jo," I say. "I'm out of here, baby doll. I've got to feed all of my cats and dogs. Back to the zoo I go. And besides, tomorrow is garbage day. I've got to take all of the canned food out of the cans for the animals and wash the trash cans," Jo says.

"Jo, you're so weird," I say. "But I love you." I hug her. "Bye, honey, I'll see you next week," she says. Jo walks out of the door.

"Bye, Jo," says Cherry. "I'm leaving this place," I say. I walk back into the locker room and pick up my purse and keys. I look in the mirror and I see the facial similarities I share with my mother. I leave the bathroom/locker room and walk out down the hall.

"I'll see you in a week," says Cherry. "I might be back," I say. "You'll be back. Everyone comes back to Iggy's. It's like an ad- diction," Cherry says. "You have my number if you need to talk."

"I have it," I say.

"Don't be afraid to use it," Cherry said. "Goodbye, Cherry,"

I said. As I walk out of the restaurant, I turn around to look at the two women immersed in their animated and cruel words. Their mouths open as their waists expand in their own Oz. I don't say goodbye to anyone else, which is so unlike me. I push open the double doors to a clear sky and to the fresh, ungreased air filling my lungs.

Eighteen

I WALK DOWN THE eroded pavement of the alley and along the backs of stores covered with bars and burglar alarms. Chipped paint and pointed bricks decorate the two-and three-storied buildings. I can feel my heart pounding in my chest and my palms perspiring. I walk in through the back door of the five and dime, and smell the aroma of salted french fries and white toast. The aisles are fat with paper towels and imitation wood grained furniture, generic crackers and mountains of hard candies in assorted flavors. I nod at the girl behind the counter standing in front of the shelves filled with radios, televisions, and assorted battery operated and digital clocks.

I push open the door and walk by the windows filled with lunch sign specials at the counter. Grilled cheese and fries with a coke are two dollars and ninety-nine cents. I can't remember what my mother looks like exactly, I thought.

I stare down at the sidewalk made from rice-sized pebbles. I have always thought of this day and what I would say. I can't let the words escape me, I thought. I cross the street, and I see an outline of a woman sitting and smoking at a table at The Sidewalk Cafe.

"Hello, Sage," she says. I stand in front of her like a child wanting an immediate answer.

"Hello," I say. "Have a seat," she says. "No," I say. "Do you want something to drink?" she asks. "No," I say. "Are you going to sit down?" she asks. "No, I don't think so," I say. "No." I stare at her coffee cup and the pink lipstick stain on the rim.

"Why'd you come?" she asks. Her sunglasses are pulled up on her head. Her longish hair is pulled back in a French knot.

"I'm not sure," I say. "You can leave," she says. "The way you did?" I ask. "Don't judge me," she says. "That's not why I came to see you."

"Then why did you come?" I ask. "I know what day this is," she says. "What is today?" I ask. I watch her sip her coffee delicately. "The anniversary of John's death. I never forget," she says.

"I don't know what you want," I say. "I want to get more coffee. Do you want anything?" she asks. "Cafe mocha," I say. "Come on," she says. She stands up and meets me eye to eye. I concede as she holds the door open for me. She stands at the counter behind a man and I stand behind her. My mother looks up at the menu.

"Can you read that?" she asks. "Yes, I can," I say. "Wait a minute," she says. She rummages in her purse and brings out an eyeglass case. She takes out a pair of eyeglasses. "That's better."

I watch her study the menu with the glasses hanging low off of her nose. The man moves and she is up at the counter. "Two cafe mochas, please," she says. "Large, please." I stand behind my mother. "Do you want anything else?" she asks. I look at the uncut coffee cake for a second too long. "We'll have two pieces of the cake," she says. "Is that all?" asks the sleepy-eyed girl with the bow tie and black pony tail.

"Anything else, Sage?" she asks. "No, nothing else," I say. I

156

watch my mother take money out of her purse and put the change back in it. She carries the tray outside; the door being held open for her by a young man coming in the cafe. She places the tray down and unloads the drinks and pieces of cake. "I'll be right back," she says.

I watch her take the tray back inside. Through the glass she pauses at the condiment counter and then walks back outside. She has silverware and napkins in her hand.

"Here you go," she says. She tucks a napkin under my plate and then places a knife and a fork on top of another napkin directly in front of me.

On a street with traffic speeding and the backfires of cars pounding against the concrete, I sit across from my mother having coffee and cake. I watch her.

"You think I want something from you, Sage, don't you?" she asks directly.

"Yes, I do," I admit. "You know everything, don't you?" she asks. "I know the truth, Mother. You see the word, Mother, doesn't even sound right coming out of my mouth. The word sticks," I snap.

"Don't judge, until you know the whole story," she says, sip- ping her drink.

"I know what I know," I say. "I can't change things," she says. "No, you can't," I say. "Your grandmother was a hard woman. She always got her way. I wasn't strong enough to stand up to her. I'm sorry for that," she apologizes.

"When I walked up to you this morning, you seemed strangely familiar. And it wasn't just the fact that we look alike, just similar. I knew who you were by your lotus pink lipstick, but there was more," I explain.

"You got my postcard?" she asks.

"Yes," I say. I take the crumbled-up postcard out of my

157

pocket. "Was this meant as a joke?"

"In my mind I wrote that postcard more than twenty years ago. I never had the courage to write it until the other day. And then I mailed it when I saw your picture in the newspaper," she says. "Why?" I ask. "Why do you want to be a mother now?" "Real life isn't like books. Sometimes there aren't any answers, and one day you wake up and you've accepted this," she says. "I wanted to make amends. You know, to resolve our relationship."

"I have all of the answers and I don't need you," I snap. "You probably don't need anyone, least of all an absent mother," she concedes.

I look at the age spots on her hands, and the significant wrinkle above her lip. She is not the same woman with the plump lips and dancing eyes. She is old. Dried skin wrinkles under her eyes, and she looks tired.

"Don't play games with me, what do you want? Money?" I ask. "I don't want anything from you, anything material anyway," she says.

"I don't think I can be a daughter. I think it's too late," I say. I take my fork and cut off a piece of cake with the side of the fork.

"Let's go about this in a different manner. I can't give to you, Mother, what I can't feel in my heart," I say.

"You're so grown up drinking coffee and fighting with words," she says. She cuts off a piece of cake with her knife and then daintily places it on her fork and into her mouth.

"That's it, I am grown up," I declare.

"I think about Rose of Sharon every day," she admits. "And I think of the day she was killed. The scene from the park plays in my head continually, and I can never purge it."

"That was a bad year," I say. "I try not to think of her. She was the closest person to me on this planet and she's gone."

"That night in the kitchen," she says. "I don't want to hear this," I interrupt. "I have to say this, Sage. That night in the kitchen, when I held your hands and we stirred the soup, I felt the pain and I knew it had to end," she says.

"Mother, what do you want from me?" I ask. "You have this rosy picture of the past. But you don't know," she says. She sips her coffee.

"What is the mystery? You left and that's it," I say dismissing her.

"Cut and dried?" she asks. "Rose of Sharon died, you left, and Daddy died, those are the facts of my life," I say. " The order of operation of my life."

"It wasn't that easy," she says. "Don't soil my memories, it's all I have," I snap. "When Rose of Sharon died, I stirred that pot of soup look- ing for some answer, at least some kind of peace. I was frozen and your father didn't help. He couldn't help me. He liked the safety of the words when he knew how the books were going to end. Your father couldn't deal with real life, and when he did, he was miserable. No, he was mean and cruel," she says.

"I don't remember that," I say. "You were young. Rose of Sharon saw what he was like. I always thought that he was glad she was killed. Rose of Sharon was old enough to question what was going on behind the walls of our bedroom," she says. "She heard my cries."

"This is what you remember," I say fiercely. "When I fell in love with your father, I didn't know that he had already pledged his love to those books, those damned books," she says. "He tolerated me because he knew I loved him and we had two small children. Sage, you have to remember things were different. Spousal abuse wasn't on the front page, it happened

159

behind closed doors. Women wore long sleeves to hide the black and blue marks."

"Why are you dragging Rose of Sharon into this?" I ask. "The night before she died, your father was reading in bed. I wanted to talk with him and just communicate. I kept asking him when he'd be done. He said one more page and this went on for an hour. You were asleep and I thought Rose of Sharon was asleep too. I sat on the corner of the bed. As a joke, I pulled the book out of your father's hands. I only wanted to get his attention and I was young. He pushed me off the bed and I hit my head on the bureau. I started crying loudly; your father stood over me and pulled back his magnificently large arm.

Rose of Sharon ran in the room and stood in front of me. I thought he would hit the both of us. I could hear your grandmother furiously scrubbing the pots and pans in the kitchen. And Rose of Sharon told him in her eight-year-old voice she'd kill him if he touched us. Your father got back in the bed and continued to read the book he had picked up from the ground," she says.

"What am I supposed to believe?" I ask. "Rose of Sharon died of an accident the very next day."

"Sometimes letting something happen is worse than doing it yourself," she says.

"Mother, I was there. Rose of Sharon went to get the ball that I dropped and she was hit by a car. If it was anyone's fault, it was mine. And I've always been sorry," I answer.

"I can see it like it was yesterday. I saw the two of you at the ice cream truck. The red ball dropped and your father was less than five feet behind you. He watched Rose of Sharon go get the ball and he turned to watch the traffic. It all happened so fast. I saw her little body hit the windshield and go straight up

160

in the air. Your father walked down the row of parked cars and picked up the red ball out of the gutter. I sat at the park table frozen. He brought me the ball and smiled," she says.

"But you left," I say. "Sage, I had a breakdown. In the middle of the bread aisle in that store, among the neon-outlined features of our neighbors, I had a breakdown. Your father visited me in the hospital that night. I was in the hospital bed, with my arms strapped down. And your father came in and read one line from Of Mice and Men. The same line over and over again. I can still hear it in the still, blackness of the night. 'George shot Lenny, and Slim comes up to him. "Never you mind," said Slim. "A guy got to sometimes."'," she said. "It sent chills through me as I watched the smile on your father's face."

"How can I believe you?" I ask. "By the time I got out of the hospital, your father was dead. I think the guilt killed him, letting his little one die within his grip. Rose of Sharon was so sweet," she says.

"I always knew she was your favorite," I say.

"She needed me more than you did," she says. "But when I look at you, I see myself and it scares me. I never want you to live through what I did. In the middle of the night, I wake up. And just for a split second, I can smell the tea roses that Rose of Sharon loved so."

"But you never came back for me. I always dreamed that you'd come back and save me," I reply.

"I knew you were strong, Sage. You've always had a wise quality, an instinct. You didn't need to be saved," she says. "You have always had an inner wisdom, Sage."

"And I tried to be in your life. I rented the house down the street from your grandmother's house. That day I saw you in the store, I knew who you were. You didn't have any idea of my identity. My hair was short and I didn't wear any makeup. I was so happy when I drove you home. You didn't question me, you trusted me," she says.

"I figured that out in the alley this morning. I remembered who you were," I say.

"And when your grandmother came out to the car. She wasn't going to let you go. She lost John and wanted someone else around. She told me she would tell the court I had abandoned you, and they would never give me custody. I was young and I believed her. Your grandmother would walk up the street and beat on my door; she said I would never get to be close to you because of what happened to Rose of Sharon. I finally gave up and left when she pulled all of the pink geraniums out of the window boxes. The look in her eyes scared me and I wasn't strong enough," she says. "When I sold candy, she wouldn't let me knock on your door. But when I came back from summer camp, you were gone. If you really wanted me, you could have fought for me," I reply.

"Things aren't what they always appear to be. Your grandmother knew the lady who owned the house and threatened her. I had to leave," she answers.

"You could have come back for me, Mother," I demand.

"When I broke down in the bread aisle, I showed my weakness. And your grandmother wouldn't tolerate weakness. She wanted me to feel the pain, but she didn't want to see it on my face," she says.

An ambulance speeds down the street, and I make the sign of the cross. My mother looks at me.

"If you search your heart, you'll find the answers," she says magically.

"I don't know what you want from me. Why did you wait so long? I still live at Grandma's house. I've always been there," I

162

say. "It got easier. I would drive by the house. Sometimes I would drive and park on Montana Street. I would watch you water the lawn and play with the dog. You remind me so much of myself at your age. You're so beautiful and you don't even know it. It's such a humble beauty; it's charming," she says.

"It's too late," I say. "You can walk away. There are no obligations. I just wanted to see you and talk to you. Call it a post-motherly concern," she says.

"I don't know how I feel," I say. "I know," she says. "No, you don't," I say. I light up a cigarette with a match and throw the match on the ground.

"Bad habit," she says. "I know. But I've got a lot of shit, right now. Why are you lecturing me?" I ask.

"I'm sorry, it's a mothering instinct," she says. "I know. I have the same thing. I do it with my dog, Steinbeck. I want to save him from bad things," I say. "Have you been honest with me? I mean are you going to tell me that something terrible is going to happen to you? Is this going to be some ironical twist that I wouldn't care for?" I ask.

"Are you going to the cemetery? I know you go every year and on holidays," she says.

"How would you know?" I ask. "Honestly?" she asks. "Yes, mother," I say. "I park over on All Saints Lane and watch for you. I watch you reading and talking to the gravestones. You have the innocence of a little girl when you read from the books. That was a very good part of him that you got," she admits.

"I've always thought I was being watched at times, but I figured it was paranoia," I say.

"It wasn't," she says. "You're not going to answer my question about your health, are you?" I ask.

"They're doing tests," she says. "They're not sure." "I don't need this shit right now," I say pointing my finger at her. "This has been a very bad day. I have to go."

I see her hand shake slightly as she takes a piece of paper out of her purse. She writes something down on the paper.

"Take this," she says. "If you need anything, well you know."

"Yes, ma'am," I say taking the paper. "Remember," she says. "I know. I have to go," I say. I walk away from the table. She looks like a china doll with her lotus pink lips and soft, wrinkled Dresden complexion.

"If you need anything, just call," she yells. She stands up and walks over to me. She opens up her petite arms and hugs me. I rest my head on her shoulder for five seconds. And then I walk away.

Nineteen

MY HEAD THROBS AND I feel a pounding behind my eyes. I walk to my car, get in it and I find myself on the freeway. I drive through the concrete jungle, palm fronds dancing above as the wind tickles them with affection. People drive past me looking in my window. I drive slowly. I get off on Glendale Boulevard. I have to see if the lotuses are blooming.

As I park my car in front of the Amy Semple Macpherson Temple, I smell burning cobs of corn from a vendor selling on the street. In the distance, I see the pink blooms. They are tall stems, with the blooms reaching their petals out to the sky.

I walk to the water, and stand in the same spot Rose of Sharon and I had been on that day. There is an irony as I look at the blooms which are within my reach now. I hold my hand out and snap a bloom. The clear gel oozes on my hand. There are fine brown lines on the bloom. Then I snap off two more blooms and hold all three in my hands. They aren't as perfect as I remember. I walk back to the car. A bell chimes as a man on the street sells mangos from his shop- ping basket. I drive away.

And I think about my father.

After Rose of Sharon was dead, my mother was gone, and my grandmother was out, I wanted to have a tea party. I asked my father if

165

he would attend; he lifted his nose up from the book and mumbled "yes."

I carried my small table and two chairs down the back stairs and onto the broken concrete below the spider web clothesline. There wasn't a tablecloth to fit my small table, so I used my grandmother's lace pillow cases. I had my white porcelain tea-pot with the light and dark pink roses on it. And it had matching cups and plates for cookies.

I set up my tea party. And I delivered my invitation to my father. Obligingly he walked down the stairs holding the book with his right hand and the handrail with his left hand.

"Here you go, Daddy," I said. "Here, little one?" he asked. "Yes, Daddy," I said. He sat in the tiny chair with his knees stuck to his chest. The book was in his hand.

"Good afternoon, sir," I said. "Hello," he said. His face was in the book.

"Fine weather, isn't it?" I asked. "Yes," he mumbled. "I'm just so busy. I have so many things to do," I said. "Yes," he said. He didn't look up at me. He stayed in the pages. "Would you like some tea? It's not really tea, but Kool-Aid. That's all we had in the refrigerator," I said.

"Huh?" he asked. "Do you want something to drink?" I asked him. "What Sage?" he asked. "Daddy, do you want something to drink?" I asked. "Yes," he said. "Daddy, you're not playing the game," I said. "Sage, I'm reading," he said. "What are you reading?" I asked. "A story," he mumbled. "Who's it by?" I asked. "You know I only read Steinbeck, Sage," he said. "Daddy, I'm having a tea party," I said. "I know, little one," he said. "But Daddy, you're not playing with me," I whined. "Sage, don't whine," he said. "But Daddy," I said. "Just let me finish the rest of this story, The Chrysanthemums, OK baby?" he asked me.

"Daddy, I want to have my tea party," I said. "Please." "Just a few more pages," he said. "No, Daddy," I said. I grabbed the book out of his hands and threw it down on the ground.

"Why did you do that?" he screamed. "I just wanted to get your

attention," I said. "Don't ever do that!" he screamed. He stood up and towered over me as he kicked the little chair out of his way.

"But, Daddy," I pleaded. "I don't want to play your stupid game," he screamed. "I'm sorry, Daddy," I whispered. "What did you say?" he screamed "I'm sorry," I whispered again. He stood over me like a giant. The book was face down on the broken concrete patio, pages stuck in muddy dirt.

"Look what you did!" he screamed. "I didn't mean to," I cried. "You're just like your mother!" he screamed. "Daddy," I cried. "Please, Daddy. I'm sorry." "You've ruined the book!" He knocked over the small table with his big hand. My china set toppled onto the concrete. Bright pink Kool-Aid ran all over the lace and the broken bits and pieces of the china set.

"Just like your mother, you cry. Another weak female!" he screamed.

"I'm sorry, Daddy," I cried. "I'll try to stop crying. I promise." He stood over me and moved his right hand back. I could see his hand trembling as he pulled it by his left side. I saw the anger in his eyes.

"John!" my grandmother screamed out from the top of the stairs. "Not again!"

My father picked up his book out of the mud and wiped it on his brown corduroys as he walked up the stairs. My grandmother tapped him on the shoulder as he walked by her, and then she disappeared through the back door and into the house.

I sat with my broken china set on the concrete in the back yard until all of the clouds had flown by me and the sky was littered with tiny flecks of light secretly whispering the promise that my mother would come home and save me.

A single tear falls from my face as I turn down the off ramp and finish the one block drive to the cemetery. I enter the gates and see the bright green grass and blooming rose bushes. I sit in the car and watch an old man turning on the water faucet above the concrete trash bin.

He walks over to a gravestone and puts flowers on the headstone. He kneels on one knee. He bows his head and puts a straw hat which was resting on the grass back on his head. Then he turns around and walks away.

I get out of the car with my book and flowers, and walk over to where the flowers sit on top of the grave.

Baby Delphin November 10, 1947 Our Baby

I want to cry for a child who is loved so much. I make the sign of the cross and I walk away. The gravestones of my sister, father and grandmother draw me like a magnet. I stand over the adjective-less gravestones and place a lotus on each one.

"What a day," I say. "You three wouldn't believe the day I've had. I think it's like the longest most traumatic day. You're my three little ghosts. And I bet you're wondering why I didn't bring flowers. I'm sorry, but I had to work today. I'll make it up to you next time."

I feel as if I'm being watched. I turn around and a station wagon slowly drives up the hill.

"Well, I do believe I'm going to read from The Long Valley today. The story is called The Chrysanthemums and we know the author," I say.

I sit down and feel the dampness from the fresh cut grass through my trousers. I read silently the first paragraph to myself. And then I read to them from the book.

"'It was a time of quiet and of waiting. The air was cold and tender. A light wind blew up from the southwest so that the farmers were mildly hopeful of a good rain before long; but fog and rain do not go together,'" I read to my audience of granite, words, and numbers.

I look at the overgrown ivy and how it conquers everything in its path. The beautiful veined leaves look so elusive. They have an innocent beauty, I think. The sun shines on my body and makes me feel warmly alone. I sit Indian style, paying homage to my family. The grass is almost flat over where they buried my grandmother in her beloved earth.

I sit and read the story silently to myself. The air smells fresh and I can barely make out the noise of the traffic through the thick of the ivy along the fence.

"I think I should share the last line with all of you. What do you think?" I ask as if I expect to hear an answer.

"'She turned up her coat collar so he could not see that she was crying weakly—like an old woman.' Isn't that beautiful? I think it is. Daddy, you never let me cry for my sister or my mother," I say.

I look around at the flowered graves in this terribly sad place. Graves which have more words than I ever heard my father speak in his lifetime. I cry for my sister and the lost half I feel when I see sisters smile and sisters laugh. I cry for my father who had no ability to live in the world in a kindly manner. I cry for my grandmother who cursed me when I frequently used the word "Why" and blushed when I asked about the rites of passage of a girl's body to an adult woman's body, from training bras to menstruation. I cry for my grandmother who silently passed me in the hall the first time I stayed out all night long and came back home smelling of cigarettes, beer, and sex. She was so old she only had her faith in the church and finished her life answering all of my questions with the definition of it being "Another mystery of the faith." I cry for my mother and the fact that I have become her. On this small bluff surrounded by the city, I cry for myself and the weakness in my character which allowed me to view existence as a positive alternative to living.

I walk to the car and look behind, because I will return. Grandma always said if you turn around and look back, you'll return.

I drive home by the freeway, listening to the bumps outlining my lane and not really seeing where I'm going.

I live with sainted memories.

Twenty

IN THE WHITENESS OF the morning, I wake up under something. It Steinbeck's thick and hairy paw. I look at the sun shine yellow through the lace curtains and at the ruby red clock scream- ing eight-ten. I stretch my body under the sheets and turn over on my stomach. Steinbeck jumps off the bed and wags his tail creating an air current.

"Five more minutes, Steinbeck," I say. He wags his tail quicker when he hears his name. "You're not going to let me sleep, are you?" I ask. Steinbeck jumps up on the bed and begins licking my face.

"No," I say, pushing him away. "Just five more minutes, please."

He looks at me with those sweet eyes. Hanging off the bed, I touch his soft coat. His heat spot has healed and new fuzzy growth is there, like a baby chick.

"Let's go," I say getting out of bed. I walk down the hallway behind Steinbeck. His paws scrap- ing the hardwood as he dances furiously in front of me. He slides across the kitchen tiles, almost running into the door as he tries to get out.

"There you go," I say. Steinbeck runs down the stairs and is gone, lost in the foliage of camellia bushes and sword ferns.

I walk back into the kitchen, and look at the remnants of

last night. A white linen tablecloth with a large burgundy wine stain. Two wine glasses, two plates, and silverware sit on the table. I plug in the coffee maker and grind beans while Steinbeck chases birds outside in the garden and barks at them. I put coffee in the filter, pour the water in the machine, and push the button. The aroma fills the kitchen and I sit at the table thinking about last night.

I went to the store and bought groceries, something I hadn't done in so long. I purchased a jar of spaghetti sauce, a box of noodles, a bag of lettuce, a bottle of wine and a crusty baguette of sourdough. When I got home, I boiled water, cooked the sauce, and dumped the bag of lettuce into a salad bowl. I overcooked the noodles and almost set a fire putting a not quite out cigarette in the trash can. I was nervous. It had been two months since my mother had come back into my life.

Steinbeck watched me as I took dress after dress out of my closet. Looking for the right dress, I realized what an influence Tomas had in my life. All of my dresses were large floral numbers with long sleeves and high necks. "Shouldn't advertise what's not for sale," he would say with a proprietary smile on his face. All of my shorter skirts and dresses had been slowly replaced by ones with hems just above my ankles or below my knees. The only dress I recognized purchasing for myself was a sleeveless A-line linen dress in vanilla. I wore that at my college graduation, it was a suitably classic choice. I put on the pearls my grandmother had given me. I looked smart.

When I walked out into the front room, I stubbed my toe on a box. The dining room was full of the boxes I had brought from storage. I had decided to go through the boxes and give away what I wouldn't use. The boxes nearly touched the old stucco on the ceiling. I sat in the big black chair and waited for my mother to ring the bell that didn't ring, but whined like a run- over cat. The light was insulated by the lace curtains in the small room. The bell whined. I walked to the door and answered it.

"Come in," I said. "Thanks," she said. "It feels the same." "Now it

feels like home to me," I announce. "Well it should, Sage. It's the only home you've ever had and known," she said. "The place looks good; time hasn't changed anything about the house," she said walking past me.

"I wasn't kidding about the boxes. I told you there were a lot. I haven't had the time to go through them. Grandma saved every- thing. There are jars filled with buttons, bric-brac, and zippers, and hundreds of unpaired eyelet hooks in baby food jars," I said.

"They're probably baby food jars from you or Rose of Sharon. That woman saved everything," she said. "She didn't want to feel she had missed out on anything."

"There are two cases of dried out tape. I don't know where she got it from," I said. "Come on in and have a seat." "You still have it," she said looking at the chair. "The same one," I said. She walks over to it and touches the armrest. She runs her hand over it and up across the back of it.

"The chair," she said. "Dad's chair," I said. I watch her sit in the chair and close her eyes. For a minute, her mind drifts back to the past and the beauty of her youth.

"It looks unused," she said running her finger along the armrest. "After he died, Grandma didn't want anyone to sit in it. She cleaned the chair religiously every week. I have good memories of that chair. I don't think I'll ever be able to part with it," I said. "Your grandmother was religious in a pagan manner," she said instantly. "And I believe the tape was from your grandfather." "What could he have done with all of that tape?" I asked. "Sage, I believe that was from his last shipment. He skimmed it off the top of the load, before he brought the shipment in," she said.

"What did he do?" I asked. "Grandma didn't talk about him. I know when I was younger she had their wedding picture on her dresser. I asked her about it. She ignored me, and I never saw the picture again."

"He was a trucker and the tape was from his last load. He wasn't home much. He was on the road most of the time. Your father only had a

173

handful of memories of him. Sage, have I told you how lovely you look?"
she asked.

"Come into the kitchen, I've set the table in there," I said changing the
subject.

As she follows me into the kitchen, she notices the armoire, which has
always been in this house.

"It's still here. I didn't think she'd get rid of it," she said. "It has a
special beauty."

"The armoire?" I asked. "I always thought she was afraid of it. She
looked at it like it had eyes and it recorded every move she made. Where
are my manners? Do you want something to drink?" I asked.

"What are you drinking?" she asked. "Burgundy," I said. "I'll have
the same," she said moving the wine glass toward me.

"Just let me open this," I said struggling with the wine bottle. "I knew
I should have gotten a bottle of wine with a twist off top. Tomas always
did this and I never learned. I always watched like it was some transitional
adult secret and I wasn't old enough."

"Here, let me show you," she said standing up. "Point it away from
you and pull gently yet firmly." She pulled the cork out of the bottle.
"What's a mother for, but to teach you life's little secrets."

"Why are you so interested in Grandma's armoire?" I asked. "Sage,
it was mine," she said. "Yours?" I asked. "Well, it was ours, your
fathers and mine," she said.

"That's funny. I can never remember him paying that much attention
to it. The only piece of furniture he cared about was that chair. He was
fanatical about the chair," I said.

"We got the chair and the armoire on our honeymoon. We went up to
Monterey, because he wanted to show me Cannery Row. It was the most
marvelous week. I remember going into the antique shop. I followed him
as he picked up trinkets and set them back down. And then he saw the
armoire, with its blonde wood and curved handles. He was so in love with
me. He said the armoire reminded him of me with its blonde tone and

graceful curves. And I looked to the right of the armoire and there was the chair. It was manly and strong, just like your father. The leather was buttery soft, and when I sat in it I felt his warm em- brace. It symbolized all of the love I had for him. I told him every time he sat in the chair, he would feel my soft cheeks and sweet kisses, and all of the love I had for him wrapped up in the black leather. That was a hundred years ago and another lifetime," she said.

"I'm sorry, I didn't know," I said. How could I know that the symbols of my mother's and father's love for one another, still exist, I thought.

"We drove home with a trailer behind our old car. I sat next to your father, practically on his lap on that old bench seat. And then everything changed when we got back here. Your grand- mother was a strong woman. She was stronger than I was. I was his wife and lover, but she was his mother," she said.

I look at my mother and I realize that she is the ballerina stuck in the musical snow globe I received on the last birthday I spent with her. The snow kept falling on the pink ceramic tutu.

"My life is like a connect the dots game, and I've never been able to finish the game. I could never get it right," I said.

"You're like your father. He was a thinker. He was a dreamer too, until we came back to this house. Then he was a reader, lost in those damned words," she said. "What have you made for dinner?" she asked.

"Spaghetti, salad, and bread," I said. "I overcooked the spaghetti, so it's not very good."

"Why do you qualify everything?" she asked. "It's what I did with him. I was like a child." I said scooping out a plate of spaghetti. "How much sauce do you want?" I asked.

"A lot of sauce, please. Can I help you with anything, Sage?" she asked.

"No, Mom I'm fine," I said. What an automatic response, I thought. "Sage, what did you call me?" she asked. "I called you Mom," I said seeing the smile in her eyes. I place the plate in front of her.

"That's so sweet. I never thought I'd hear you call me that again. I've always felt like a mother, but it's been so long since I felt like a mom," she said. "Thanks, Sage."

"Let me get my plate and I can join you. I'm sorry. I don't have any cheese. I forgot, I'm sorry," I said.

"Why do you apologize so much? It's no big thing. We can go without," she said.

"I did it with, Tomas. It's a habit, a hard one to break," I said.

I walk to the table with my plate and sit down.

"I've waited for this day, and I always believed it would hap- pen," she said. "The table looks wonderful. And the bread looks too beautiful to break."

"I remember one of the last things you said to me, Mom. You said you were going to get bread for the table," I said.

"Those words meant so much more. I never realized the symbolism of such a simple sentence. Sage, the words make us who we are and our pasts make us who we are today," she said.

I looked at my mother and I smiled. "I didn't think you'd call me and especially not the same day I dropped in on you. Have you heard from him since that night?" she asked.

"It's funny," I said. I pick up the baguette, tear off a piece, and place it on my plate. "I knew you for five years and then you were gone. I knew Tomas for five years and now he's gone. And you're back in my life," I said.

"Can I ask you what happened? I mean I know you called me that night, but why?" she asked.

I watch my mother break off a piece of bread and wipe the crumbs from the tablecloth. She stands up and throws the crumbs in the trash, and then returns to her seat.

"When I came home from the cemetery, I was so tired. I walked into the house. In the afternoon darkness, I reached under the bathroom cabinet. The pregnancy test was negative and I was so overjoyed. I was just

176

happy that I wouldn't have a life connection to Tomas," I said.

"So, you weren't pregnant. And that was the key?" she asked. "Existence. I was just existing. Mom, I wasn't living. Do you know what that's like?" I asked.

"Yeah, Sage, I do," she said. I looked at her and she knew. She did the same. I did the same, I thought. We were closer than I ever wanted to believe.

"I looked through the armoire that afternoon. I was looking for something. I think a pair of scissors. I found a journal. In it there were Grandma's words. All of the hatred she kept bottled up was written down in those pages," I said.

"I knew she had a book. I found it one day and began to read it. I read all about Miss Abigail and all of the hatred she had for the woman. Your grandmother caught me reading it and she ripped it out of my hands," she said. "She was such a secretive person. She told me I invaded her privacy and she would never forgive me."

"I didn't know Miss Abigail lived down the street in the pink and white house," I said. "Her address and phone number were in the book. Grandma documented everything she did to Miss Abigail and you in the book."

"When I got out of the hospital, Miss Abigail was the only person I could think of to help me. Your father was dead and I had no friends or relatives. I remember walking up to the house and knocking on the door. This attractive older woman walked up the driveway. She invited me into her back house. She lived in the back house. She had a Southern accent, and enchanted me over tea and biscuits. Miss Abigail knew who I was; she had seen me and knew I lived down the street. I remember sitting on the sofa surrounded by boxes of old gummy tape. They were all she had left of her past. In the small room, she explained to me that I could never win with your grandmother. She had tried and lost. All of the love she had for your grandfather was insulated by the boxes of tape. You know Miss Abigail was your grandfather's first wife," my mother said.

177

"Grandma was very detailed in her journal," I said. "I knew he was divorced and that was practically unheard of at the time. But your grandmother wanted to marry him and she did," she said.

I watch my mother daintily twirl her fork in the spaghetti. "Your grandmother always got what she wanted. Miss Abigail lived in fear of her. She lived in the back house. The front house was a museum to your grandfather. She walked me into the house and it smelled musty. I remember Miss Abigail and her slow ladylike walk. And the dainty way she held the back door open for me. She never said one word about your grandfather and I never asked. Miss Abigail said she would let me live there, as long as I promised not to disturb anything," she said.

"But you left," I said. "Your grandmother found out I was living there. She hated Miss Abigail. She hated her despite the fact that she gave your grandfather a divorce. Your grandfather thought he had fallen in love with your grandmother. I think he was always sorry he divorced Miss Abigail. I think they had a special love. He visited her, because he was still in love with her. Your grandfather was forty-seven by the time your father was born. Miss Abigail was a broken woman, because your grandfather was her only love. She would tell me how he would come down there and they would relive their past. He died in the house down there. Miss Abigail said he died in the rocking chair. During the last afternoon tea, he said he just needed to catch his breath. He closed his eyes and died when the rocking stopped. Your grandmother never forgave her. She said she never let go. Miss Abigail let me stay in that front house. The only catch was that I had to sit in the chair and gain my strength from the memory of the man she loved. She wanted to hear the creaking from the chair as she hung out her laundry. Her personals, as she called them, weren't hung out; just sheets and towels, dresses and blouses," she said.

"But, Mom, you left," I said. "I left because your grandmother threatened to burn down the house. It was the only thing Miss Abigail had left of him, so I left. I had no choice. She said I would never win against your grandmother. Miss Abigail knew from experience. I knew *from experience. I'd lost your father. Miss Abigail said you'd understand one day. She whispered those words into my ear as I walked out of the house. I didn't have the strength to look back at the woman who mumbled to his ghost and tenderly spoke to the boxes of tape every evening, when she read the newspaper into thin air," she said.*

"You left because you had to, I read her anger in her journal," I said. "I kicked Tomas out because I had to. He would have never left me."

"You scared me when you called me that night," she said. "I was scared," I said. "I remember when Tomas came home that night. I was happy. And when he asked me why I was so happy, I told him it was because I wasn't pregnant. He turned to me and gave me a back-handed slap which sent me to the floor."

"You were crying when you called me, Sage," she said. "I need more wine, let me just reach the bottle, damn," I said. The wine bottle tipped over and spilled on the white linen tablecloth.

"I'll get something," she said. She walked over to the paper towels. "Here we go," she said wiping up the spilled wine. "It's not much of a mess. A little soaking and it'll be like new."

I look at my mother and I wonder how I picked up so many of her habits and mannerisms since I only knew her the first five years of my life.

"I called you that night when he was outside pounding on the door. I locked him out of the house when he went to take the trash out," I said.

"Do you love him, Sage?" she asked. "I loved what I thought was love," I said. "I was crying when I called you and you told me to calm down. I remember hearing him scream outside the front doors. The windows rattled as he screamed he'd huff and he'd puff and he'd blow this house down. The only reason he left was because Mrs. Church threatened to call the police. She was screaming at him from her front porch with a baseball bat in her hand. She's a tough old woman."

"Yes she is. When your father would scream and yell at me in the bedroom, I always felt I was being watched. One night from across the gully, she whispered to me to leave, to get out. She told me your grandfather

had done the same to your grandmother until she found the power of the cast iron skillet. But then everything fell apart with Rose of Sharon, and I felt I had no control. I wasn't strong enough. I didn't want the same thing to happen to you. I always believed you were too smart for anything to happen to you like that. But when you were crying on the phone, I knew," she said. "I knew something was terribly wrong, sins of the mother coming back on you."

"I was crying," I trailed off into silence. "Are you all right, Sage?" she asked. "And then you asked me if I wanted you to come over here. You sounded like a mother and that was all I needed," I said.

"I am your mother," she whispered. "He won't give up," I said. "Do you know that his stuff fit into two boxes? We were together for five years, and there were just two boxes. I don't think he'll ever understand how he hurt me."

"Sage, you have to let it go." "The next day I went to the store, I wasn't gone that long. When I came home, the front door was open. I walked into the house, and I thought Grandma was on the floor gathering pa- pers. It was Mrs. Church, but she looked just like her. She was on her knees gathering pages. Tomas had waited until I left, and then he went into the house. He ripped apart all of Daddy's books, tore all of the pages off of the spines. She had chased him away with her baseball bat, but only after he'd ruined all of the books. She was sorry she hadn't been able to stop him. I sat in the front room crying for my loss of perfection and the destruction of the words. I had fallen under the same spell, the beauty in the words," I said.

"I'm sorry, Sage. I know how much his books meant to you, they were your only link to him," she said.

"He did me more of a favor than he'll ever know. As I sat there crying, I realized I could never go back to the way it was. I didn't want to go back. It was too late," I said.

"He did you a favor, through his cruelty," she said. "I can't explain it, but it's something you feel in your heart," I said.

180

"When I left that night, I looked at you standing on the chair in the kitchen. You were sweetly stirring the soup in the kitchen. I looked back at you as I walked out the door to go to the store. Your head was bent low under the naked bulb, and you looked almost like an angel. And I told you to stir because I was going to get bread for the table. Do you remember?" she asked.

"I never forgot," I said. "Those words meant so much more," she said. "Mom," I said. I look at my mother's face. She has her pain and I have my pain. A common bond, I thought.

"There are things in life you just have to do. Let your hair down and take a chance. You aren't alone," she said.

I look at my mother sitting across from me at the table. There are things in life I just have to do, I thought.

The coffee finishes brewing. I stand up and pour myself a cup, and then I sit back down. I look across the kitchen, to the journal my grandmother kept. And I believe my mother and all of the words she shared. My grandmother's hatred toward Miss Abigail and my mother is in black and white, littering the pages of the journal.

The phone rings. "He doesn't live here anymore and I don't know where he is," I said picking it up and not listening to any more questions.

I look into my cup of coffee and I think about Delmar.

I walked into the deli after my week off when the sky had cleared up. Things hadn't physically changed. It still looked like a coffee shop in a Vegas hotel. Delmar wasn't in the garage, but his basket was.

"Where's Delmar?" I asked, without saying good morning. "Delmar's dead," Matty said between bites of her cinnamon danish.

"How?" I asked. "He got into a fight with another guy over the coat he wore. The guy pushed him down and he hit his head on a concrete parking barrier. He was still wearing the coat," she said.

I stand in the deli feeling disconnected. Lulu walks over to me.

181

"Are you ready to play now?" she sneered. "Excuse me," I said. "Are you ready to play by our rules," she said. "We have rules that must be adhered to. If you don't like it, quit."

"I see you haven't changed," I said. "I don't have the problem," she snapped. "If I asked you to step in front of my car so I could test my brakes, would you oblige?" I asked.

"I'm gonna tell Miss Lee," she said. "Fuck off, Lulu," I said. "You're fired," she screamed. Lulu walked away with a smile on her face.

I sit in the kitchen looking at the coffee, remembering Delmar. Everyone serves a purpose, I think.

Steinbeck barks outside and someone is knocking on the front door. I walk to the door and open it.

"More?" I ask. "Yes, ma'am," the guy says. "Same guy?" I ask. "It doesn't look like he's giving up, ma'am," the guy says. "Wait a minute," I say. I walk to the couch and pull a couple of bucks out of my wallet. "Here you go."

"Thanks, ma'am," he says. "I'll probably see you tomorrow." The flower delivery guy walked to his van, and drove down the street. I hold the flowers in my hand and bend over to pick up the newspaper. I look at the houses and think how fresh they look at this time of the morning. I haven't been home at this time of the morning since I was on summer vacation, I think.

"Pink, yellow, white, and purple. He never sends red, the true color of the expression of love," I say.

I open the card. The same message. "Dance with me forever." I walk into the house and put the flowers on top of the boxes. The dried-out arrangements litter the cardboard and make a garden. The perfume is suffocating.

The phone rings and I walk into the kitchen to answer it. I sit at the table with my coffee and pick it up.

'Hi, Mom," I say. "I enjoyed last night." "More flowers,

same message." "I'll be all right. I can handle it." "Talk to you later, bye Mom," I say hanging up the phone. I sit at the table, and reach across to the counter for the bright red apple. I take a few bites and leave the apple on the table. I can leave it here and nothing will happen, I think.

Steinbeck walks in the door and to his water bowl. He slurps water and sits on the floor scratching his fleas. Then he walks back out of the door.

I walk to the back porch and sit next to Steinbeck. So much has happened in this garden, I think.

The phone rings. I walk inside to pick it up. "Yes, Rosemary," I say. "They'll be done. I got it, fifty pairs. I'm gonna start today. I can do it. I'll call you when I finish the earrings, bye."

I hang up the phone and walk back to the back porch. "What a garden, huh?" I ask Steinbeck. Steinbeck jumps from his place and runs down the stairs chasing birds.

I walk down the stairs and feel the ghostly memories. The perfume from the roses floats through the air. The pages from the books sit in a box under the blue sky. One day I'll be able to part with my vine doodled pages, but not right now. There's only so much I can do in a day.

The windshield I got from the junkyard rests against the spider web clothesline. I pick up my plastic goggles and the sledgehammer. The windshield is in the box. I stand on the broken concrete and swing at the windshield in the brown moving box. It shatters inside the box.

"What are you doing, Sage?" asks Mrs. Church through the chain link fence.

I can see the outline of her face through the rose bushes and poinsettia blooms.

"I'm creating," I answer.

"It sounds like you're destroying," she says. "Sometimes you have to break things down in order to build them back up," I say.

"You've always been a strange one, but I understand," she says. She walks back up her stairs and into her house.

"You have a good morning, Mrs. Church," I yell at her closed door.

I look at all of the broken, jagged pieces in the box. I can see the earring designs in my head. They all make sense. Angry, flower-like designs made from the memories of my family.

I look at the dried out rose buds fallen to the ground under the rose bushes; and I realize they existed, but were never able to bloom. I can bloom now because I live.

Thank you for reading
Bread for the Table

Feel free to share your thoughts by leaving a review for
Bread for the Table, *at:*

Tara Botel Doherty On

Facebook

Amazon

GoodReads

For more information on Tara Botel Doherty
Visit www.tarabotedoherty.com

Tara Botel Doherty
Bread for the Table

Tara Botel Doherty is a native of Los Angeles. She was raised by her grandmother and mother blocks away from Hollywood Boulevard. She holds an MPW from USC. Now residing up in the Santa Clarita Valley with her husband and daughter, she writes regularly about her adventures in Hollywood. *Bread for the Table* is her first novel.

Study Guide Questions for Bread for the Table

1.) Who are the key characters? What does Sage look like? Is there an absence in her physical description? Are the voices believable in this story? Does the mother sound real? Do you empathize with the characters? Are their voices genuine, are they believable? For example, does the child narrator sound the age he or she should be?

2.) What style is it written in? Is it third, or first person, or (what is rarely) written in second (you)?

3.) What is the book about? Does the book have a central theme? If so, what?

4.) Where does the book take place? Have you ever been to this neighborhood? Do you know anyone who lives there? Or, is it a nice place for a visit, only?

5.) What did you like or dislike? Explain with an example from the text.

6.) What do you think happens a week, a month, or even a year after the novel takes place?